She left that sadness behind. Dropped it on the mountains below. This was no time for feeling despair about her world.

She was alive and living in the air.

Skye slowed, rolled and spun as she flew, luxuriating in the freedom of her wings.

There was nothing like it. An updraft of wind caught her and she canted her right wing slightly and dove. Just for fun.

It was then she felt the trap enclose her.

She hit the edge of the box hard, and it tightened around her, making her crouch into the small space. Her head throbbed with pain. It was so thick, she couldn't tell if the pain was from hitting the cold iron box or if it was just because of the cold iron.

Skye could see nothing outside the blackness. Could feel it, hard and hot, closed around her. Tightening, until she touched all sides of it while crouched.

Also by Linda Jordan:
Notes on the Moon People
Falling Into Flight
Infected by Magic
Aboard the Universe
Living in the Lower Chakras
Bibi's Bargain Boutique

Coming Soon:
The Bones of the Earth Book 2: Faerie Contact
The Bones of the Earth Book 3: Faerie Descent
The Bones of the Earth Book 4: Faerie Flight
The Bones of the Earth Book 5: Faerie Confluence

Come on over to Linda's website and join the fun!
www.LindaJordan.net

Don't miss a release!
Sign up for Linda's Serendipitous Newsletter while you're
there

Faerie Unraveled

The Bones of the Earth:

Book 1

Welcome to Faerie Bella ∘

Linda Jordan

Published by Metamorphosis Press
www.MetamorphosisPress.com

ISBN-13: 978-0692661079/ISBN-10: 0692661077

The Bones of the Earth

Book 1:

Faerie Unraveled

BY

LINDA JORDAN

Metamorphosis Press

For Michael & Zoe

Chapter 1 · Skye

Skye squatted on the sidewalk beneath the bare canopy of a giant horse chestnut tree, her stretchy leggings bunching around the knees. Cars drove past periodically. She could smell their exhaust, hear their churning engines which broke the quiet of the night. But the scrawny coyote wasn't bothered by them. He glared at her, not yet ready to surrender his kill; someone's orange cat out wandering the night.

She just watched, not threatening him. Longing to be part of the night, of the wild. Along this main street in Seattle, before dawn, was about as wild as she could find in the city.

Skye knew the coyote had registered she wasn't human. Could smell the Fae on her, but wasn't sure if she was a predator. Probably never met anything like her before.

Most of Faerie had retreated from the world. Beyond caring. Drowning in their hypnotic pleasures.

The breeze blew and she caught the sweet scent of lilacs. She closed her eyes at the lovely smell. Remembering other lilacs and more gentle times. Those in Faerie.

How could Faerie leave humans to their own destruction? When the humans killed Gaia, Faerie would be destroyed as well.

Most humans had lost their connection with the Earth. They lived crammed in cities such as this one.

Forgetting the intimate place names. Forgetting the name for what a place looked like when sunlight pierced a dense woodland. Or when the breeze blew just slightly enough to lift a tree's leaves.

How could anyone forget such things?

The coyote finished his meal and scuttled down the now empty street into an alley.

She'd sought his company, but probably looked too human for his comfort.

Even though she wore a human's body, Skye was still a sylph. She'd created the human body, which surrounded her Fae self, and was living in the modern world. The human world.

A being out of place and time.

Determined to wage war on the disappearance of the old ways. Her friends no longer rode the thermals with her. She'd had to find new friends. Hawks and eagles.

Her old friends no longer walked the land with her. Now she walked with coyotes and cats.

Skye was determined to change what she could. Try to heal the Earth one human body at a time.

She straightened, feeling her muscles contract, and moved farther down the street. There were a few people walking down here in the business section.

She followed a couple of men, listening to them argue the merits of a movie they'd both seen the night before. Passed a restaurant where the smells of garlic and bacon made her mouth water. It was tempting to go inside, but human food always left her unsatisfied.

Fae didn't need to eat much. They ate mostly for pleasure. She could survive just by eating a small green leaf every day. Mostly, that's what she did, but it wasn't extraordinary like the food in Faerie.

But she wasn't going back. At least not for a very long time.

She'd chosen to do her work here. With humans.

Skye needed to make them understand how precious this Earth was. And to care for the planet, before it was too late.

Which it might be already.

A bus stopped and let two people off.

She held her breath until the bus was gone and the exhaust dissipated. Buses and old delivery trucks were the worst.

Skye stood in front of the old brick building and punched numbers into the security code box then opened the door. She climbed the stairs to the top floor, opened her door and walked into the nearly empty space.

It was an older building. With wood floors throughout. Except for the kitchen and bathroom, which were laid with slate tiles. She walked to the window and opened it, seeing clouds move swiftly across the sky.

She missed flying.

The cold wind streamed across her face.

Her wings weren't visible while she was in this form. They felt cramped inside this body she'd created, but she needed to pass for human to do her work.

Skye closed the window and turned away from it, taking in the room. A rustic brown wool rug lay in the center, beneath a large picture window which overlooked the street below and the blue and orange Fremont bridge a couple of blocks away.

11

She'd grouped three mismatched oak chairs there, around an old wooden coffee table she'd found at the local antique mall. New Age magazines lay on the smooth surface of the table. A vase of lilacs and quince sat on a low bookcase beneath the big window on that side of the room. Two other walls were covered with full size murals one of her clients had painted. One of a forest and one of a hillside with a grand vista of more hills and the sky. It made the room feel expansive.

This was her waiting room, just off the open kitchen.

In each of the two other rooms stood a massage table, a wooden chair and a small table which held her herbal oils, a small sound system to play relaxing music on and something from the natural world, a stone, a branch, perhaps a feather. And of course, a candle.

Skye took off her jacket and hung it in the closet by the front door. Then tugged on the turquoise tunic, pulling it back into place

She walked into the kitchen and poured purified water into a tea kettle and set it on the stove, turning the burner on.

She scooped green tea into the teapot and glanced out the window. The sky was coloring a lovely salmon pink. Dawn.

Her first client would be here in an hour.

She poured boiling water into the teapot, stirring the leaves with her finger, savoring the steam and heat of the water. Being in a human body always made her feel cold.

Except when she was working.

Skye went into the first room, the one with the green door, and sat on the wooden chair, removing her soft leather shoes and putting them in the closet. Her socks she tossed into the hamper.

She left her feet bare and cranked up the heat in the room. Turning on the massage table warmer, she lit the candle so it would gently scent the air. Then switched on the sound system and gentle Indian flute music began to play.

Skye turned up the heat in the blue room as well and set the warmer to turn on in an hour and a half. She closed her eyes and asked what her second client needed. The answer came back that burning sandalwood incense would be helpful. She lit a stick and put it in the holder, left the room and closed the door.

Back in the kitchen, she poured her tea and slid out the drawer which held her laptop. She checked the website and looked at her appointments for the day. She was booked solid until nine tonight. Good.

The more people she treated and helped heal, the faster the Earth could be healed. People needed to be brought back into balance.

She sipped the bright tasting tea and checked her messages. No cancellations. And three requests to be worked into the schedule early if there were cancellations. She responded to the messages, offering 9PM slots to each of those for the next several nights.

Then closed the computer and slid the drawer closed.

She didn't like using it or the cell phone. The vibrations in the air surrounding them annoyed her. It felt unpleasant. But there was no avoiding them if she wanted to do her work.

There were a few others like her. Fae who'd left Faerie to work in the world. To try to save Earth. They didn't meet often.

One was a chef in New York, another a garden designer in London, a third was a florist in Rome. Others helped people in large cities around the world, trying to reach as many people as possible. Nurses, booksellers, interior decorators, therapists, artists, environmentalists and philosophers, all working to save Earth and the humans on it.

Humanity was responding, sluggishly. It was a slow ship to turn. And it was still heading towards an iceberg.

Skye turned on some steel drum music and stretched, feeling her human body come more alive. Feeling the blood flow and her soul align once again with the planet's energy.

Being on the computer always made her disconnect from the world.

No wonder people were such a mess.

She danced, feeling the drum beats pulse through her. Thanking the universe for her life.

Then she turned off the music, poured more tea and sat in one of the chairs, waiting for her client to arrive.

He came five minutes early. Skye opened the downstairs door when he called on the little box. Then she unlocked the upstairs door.

She could hear his heavy steps on the stairs. Sadness and despair filled the air around him.

Putting her cup next to the sink, she covered the teapot with a towel to keep the tea warm.

He knocked gently and came through the door, closing it behind him.

"Good morning Gene," she said.

"Good morning," he replied, in a deep morning voice.

"Would you like some tea?"

"No, I already had coffee."

He took his coat off and hung it on the coat rack by the door.

She sat on one of the wooden chairs and he came and sat in another.

"What would you like to work on this morning?"

"I'm completely stressed out. Past my deadline on one project. Behind on others. My wife's mad at me because I missed Hannah's soccer game last night. So my daughter feels sad too, although she hid it pretty well. I shouldn't have even taken the time off to be here. But you always make me feel better," he smiled.

She could see the wounded young boy inside him. Beaten down by life.

"Okay, go on into the green room, undress and get on the table."

He nodded and walked back towards the room. His dread following him like a huge dark shadow.

Skye went to the window again, opening it and breathing the lingering fresh air from the night. She grabbed a hair tie from the drawer and pulled back the long, wavy ash blonde hair in a low pony tail at the base of her neck.

She knew what he needed. She felt the cold outside air on her human skin. She closed her eyes and sat for a minute, trying to slow her breathing. Finally, the Earth's energy flowed into her, giving her needed strength.

It was time.

Skye closed the window, went down the hall and knocked gently on the green door.

"I'm ready," he said.

She entered and closed the door. The window shades were down, letting in a minimum of light. The candle flickered on the table.

Gene was under the sheet on the massage table, lying on his belly.

She rubbed some juniper berry oil on her hands to warm them.

Then she began her magic.

Loosening his muscles, feeling the tension begin to flow away. She took that tension into her body, transmuted it and returned it to him in the form of energy.

Skye moved around the table like a dancer, pleased she'd designed this body for such athletic movement. Feeling her feet sliding across the wood floor, drawing the Earth's power up through the building like blood through veins.

Her hands felt hot from the power flowing through her.

With her Fae eyes she could see the dark spots in his body and convinced them to move where they belonged, or to leave.

She ignored the shadow in the room that hovered behind her. It would feel uncomfortable and leave or it wouldn't. She couldn't banish all his demons. He would have to do that.

She felt Gene begin to release the despair and hopelessness which accompanied him. He breathed in the fire from the candle, the water from a bowl, the fresh air from the outside which had accompanied her into the room, and the earth from the rocks which lined the windowsill.

Skye felt him come back into his body, to feel alive and hopeful again. The shadow in the room slid out between the cracks around the window.

Unwanted, it would move on to find another poor soul.

Gene had a large dark spot around his neck and she held her hands over that for a long time. Finally, the darkness dissipated and went down where it belonged. In his lower torso, to strengthen and stabilize him. His neck still looked raw. Vulnerable. She tried to fill the space with brightness and light. Enough to hold him over, until he could recharge himself.

Finally, Skye had done as much as she could.

She held her hands over his heart and said, "You must spend some time in nature to fully heal. To de-stress. I don't care how you do it. Walk during your lunchtime and see the trees, the sun, the clouds. Go to your daughter's next soccer game and feel the breeze blowing past. Go for a walk after dinner or before bed and listen to the night sounds. But go outside and smell the air. Notice plants, clouds, wind. Pick up rocks. Touch the earth. That is how you'll heal yourself."

"Thank you," he said.

She said, "Take your time getting up and dressed. I'll be out in the other room."

Skye left the room, closing the door behind her.

In the kitchen, she washed her hands with a gentle soap, dried them and poured herself another cup of tea.

Then she checked to make sure the blue room was ready. The massage table warmer had turned on and the room was filled with sandalwood incense. Perhaps a little too much. She lit the candle and left the door open to let some of the incense out, then turned on the same sound system and flute music streamed into this room as well.

Back in the kitchen, she sipped her tea, watching the clouds move across the sky.

Tonight.

Tonight she needed to leave this human body behind.

Become Fae again and fly.

Gene came out of the room, his face pink from the heat and her work. He looked lighter and carried a vibrancy about him.

"I can't thank you enough," he said, putting the money in a silver bowl on the counter.

Skye only accepted cash. She didn't have a bank account. Didn't want to have a bank account or deal with taxes. Having to explain the Fae thing wouldn't go over well. She worked with an accountant, who was one of her clients, whom she paid to take care of the internet, phone, electric bills and apartment rental.

That left her free to do her work.

Gene scheduled another appointment and left.

Skye went back into the green room, turned the heat off, opened the curtains and the window and lit some sage to clear the room of his energy.

She took the sheet off the massage table, stuffed it in the hamper, which she carried out into the hallway. Opening the door, she started the washing machine. Thank goodness the machine was quiet, so she could wash things while she had clients. Because she liked to always have clients.

Putting the hamper back in the green room, she put a clean sheet on the massage table, closed the window, then the curtains and waved the smoke from the sage around the room. She put the sage out, turned the heat back on, checked that the warmer for the massage table was on and closed the door.

Ready for the next client in that room.

Skye liked to always have the next room ready. Sometimes clients came early and it was nice to have a place set up for them to go into while she tidied up the other room. It helped her to keep people moving through seamlessly. Which kept her centered.

The door entry signal for down below rang and she opened it for Heather.

She heard Heather bounding up the stairs like a crazed child. She came in Skye's apartment and closed the front door loudly.

"Hi," she said, breathless from the stairs.

"Good morning."

Heather pulled off her hoodie and hung it on the coat rack.

"I've got some green tea, would you like some?"

"No thanks, just a glass of water," said Heather, her breathing slowing a bit.

Heather poured herself a glass of water from the pitcher of purified water which sat on the counter. She drank the entire glass at once.

As far as Skye could tell, Heather did everything that way.

"How are you this morning?"

Heather put the empty glass over by the sink.

She said, "I'm all in a jumble this morning. My life's exploding. Mom fell and broke her hip. I need to fly back there tomorrow. Jim and I are fighting. Again. Work is a mess. They're laying people off right and left. No one's job is safe. I'm not sure about mine. Everything's in chaos."

Skye nodded.

"Why don't you go into the blue room, get undressed and lie on the table. I'll be in in about five minutes."

"Great," said Heather, heading off down the hall.

What a bundle of fire she was today.

Skye opened the kitchen window to breathe in fresh air. She closed her eyes, trying to find what Heather needed most. When she had it, she closed the window and went down the hall.

She knocked gently on the door.

"I'm ready," said Heather.

Skye rubbed some lavender oil on her hands and laid them on Heather's back. Calming the energy and rearranging the priorities. Heather's energy flowed with her, allowing the changes to happen. Removing a stubborn knot here, breaking up a clog there. Skye's work allowed the person to move into the best of who they could be.

If they so chose.

Some didn't. Those returned each time with the same problems. Stuck.

Others moved through their challenges and grew towards lives that fulfilled them. Still others did some combination of both.

Skye didn't have the gift of knowing who would move forward and who would remain stuck. Sometimes she predicted correctly, other times not. Now and then a person surprised her completely. After months of being stuck, they suddenly broke free and changed.

Eventually, Heather's energy flowed smoothly and serenely. It felt balanced and strong.

Skye said, "It's important for you not to get caught up in other people's drama. You've got a lot going on right now. Take time for yourself. Leave the office at lunchtime.

Go for a walk outside. When you sense a conflict coming on with Jim, go sit out on your balcony. Breathe in the fresh air. Make sure you take care of yourself while you're caring for your mom. That will help you stay balanced and strong. Spend some time out in nature. Even if it's just looking at the moon or clouds before you go to bed."

"Thank you," said Heather.

"Take your time getting dressed."

Skye left the room and went into the kitchen. She washed her hands, feeling her own energy flowing.

The time moved quickly. One client after another. Each unique in their own problems. She did her best to help them. To reconnect them to their own energy and to the Earth. To their sustenance.

Finally, it was ten at night. The last patient gone. Everything cleaned up and ready to go for the next day. Heat turned off everywhere. Laundry all done and put away. Dishes washed.

She locked her front door. Removed her clothes and showered, a last cleansing of other people's energy.

Dried off, she opened every window in the apartment and stood in a warm robe and slippers in front of the kitchen window. A large maple stood in front of the window, making her less visible from down below.

She breathed in the fresh air, then closed all the windows except the kitchen one and took herself to the blue room. She laid down on the massage table, turning on the heater just slightly and pulling a blanket over herself. Then she slid out of her human body, leaving it behind on the table. Warm and cozy, she tucked it in to keep it warm.

And became Skye again. Her real self. The sylph. She unfolded her glorious, iridescent wings, fluttering them to dry and stretch them out. They felt stiff from idleness. Her bluish-skinned body felt light again.

Her Fae body was thinner and longer than humans'. The senses sharper. Her eyes larger, she could see colors humans couldn't. Smell things they'd never sense. Her thick knee length white hair was plaited into several braids.

She ran to the kitchen, perched on the window sill and launched herself into the maple tree, startling a pair of squirrels who lived there.

Skye jumped from branch to branch until she was higher up in the bare branched canopy. Then she soared off over the rooftops, feeling the power of her wings as they moved the air. She slid through the sky, leaving the city behind in just minutes.

The cool air felt perfect on her skin.

She flew high enough that from the ground she'd be seen as a large bird. If she was seen at all. Most people were in bed or in front of a screen at this time of night.

Skye flew west over Puget Sound, over the Olympic Mountains, towards the sea. Once past the mountains she dove down. She could feel her body pierce the air, like a falcon must experience when diving for prey. The pressure made her long hair stream out behind her. The feathers on her tucked in wings rippled. Hell, even her skin rippled.

Then Skye pulled up, stretched out her wings and beat them. Up. Down. Up. Down, surging forward. She basked in the power of her own body.

She wanted to feel the ocean wind on her body. Feel the wildness.

There was still snow on the Olympics. A lot of snow. Winter hadn't finished with this part of the world. At least not the highest peaks.

The coldness filled her with life.

Skye remembered flying with her sisters in the cold air over what would become Iceland. It had been remarkable, the ice and the colors in the sky. Her sisters now grown stupid with luxury. Retreated from the world with most of the rest of Faerie.

She left that sadness behind. Dropped it on the mountains below. This was no time for feeling despair about her world.

She was alive and living in the air.

Skye slowed, rolled and spun as she flew, luxuriating in the freedom of her wings.

There was nothing like it. An updraft of wind caught her and she canted her right wing slightly and dove. Just for fun.

It was then she felt the trap enclose her.

She hit the edge of the box hard, and it tightened around her, making her crouch into the small space. Her head throbbed with pain. It was so thick, she couldn't tell if the pain was from hitting the cold iron box or if it was just because of the cold iron.

Skye could see nothing outside the blackness. Could feel it, hard and hot, closed around her. Tightening, until she touched all sides of it while crouched.

She screamed in pain and anger.

Deep laughter answered her screams.

"Who are you? Let me go."

There was no answer.

Only more laughter.

Chapter 2 · Dylan

Dylan stood on the cliff above the Pacific. He gazed out at the unusually calm ocean, squinted his eyes and applied more Payne's gray to his brush, mixing it in with the blue paint on the palette in his left hand.

He brushed paint across the top page of the watercolor block clamped to his easel, capturing the cloud perfectly. The wind picked up a bit, blowing fine strands of hair across his face. It caught in the stubble on his cheek. He really should shave. His agent was coming this afternoon. To get the new batch of paintings.

He stopped working this one, just in time. Before he'd added too much detail.

Humans didn't like too much detail. They didn't want to see the six-pack ring wrapped around the piece of driftwood. Or the vodka bottle on the beach. The dead pieces of crab breaking down in the sun.

They just wanted beauty. And they had a very narrow definition of it.

Dylan put down his brush and breathed in deep, the smell of the sea. Fish, kelp and water. And much more than that. Seal fur. A pod of orca were feeding just out past where the ocean floor dropped off into the depths. Oil from several fishing boats that had gone out early in the morning floated in the current.

He could taste the oil, even from here. It had a chemical, solvent flavor.

Dylan stretched and packed up his paints in the light wooden case. He dumped his paint-filled water on a clump of dry looking beach grass. The paint wouldn't harm them. Put his brushes away, wrapped in plastic to keep them moist. He'd clean them thoroughly back at the studio. He folded the easel legs up, put the easel beneath his arm, being careful of the wet painting still attached to it, picked up the wooden case of paints and brushes with his free hand and trudged back through the sandy grass to the parking lot.

Dylan unlocked his bicycle from the sign post he'd chained it to earlier. He detached the watercolor block from the easel, and covered the painting, now dry from the breeze, by flipping the cover over the top of it. Then he slid the pad into one of the panniers, along with the case of paints. He folded the easel down further and slipped it into the basket on the other side.

Wiping his hands on his jeans, he brushed the long hair out of his face, regathering it in an elastic tie. He wasn't going to cut his hair. Water sprites had long hair. And even though he wore a human body these days, in order to do his work, he wasn't about to have short hair.

He got on his bike and pedaled back to the studio and his cabin. Dylan passed up the traffic sitting on the main street. The car exhaust smelled awful, making it hard to breathe.

Traffic was stuck as usual. Winter was still here, but anytime the weather was beautiful, the population of the town swelled. The streets weren't made for this many cars.

Humans and their cars.

He'd never understand.

Of course humans hadn't had the opportunities to swim the world's oceans, lakes and rivers like he had. To see the incredible beauty that existed all around them.

It was as if they were blind.

Which was why he painted. To try and help them see how glorious the world around them was.

Why did they have to go anywhere their own power couldn't take them?

The sun poked through the clouds and blazed down on him. Heating up his pale skin. He began to sweat, beneath the fleece jacket.

It took him ten minutes to get back to the studio.

He parked the bike inside the living room of the cottage and unloaded it, laying the painting out on a large table. He tossed the jacket over the back of his kitchen chair.

The cottage had been built for vacationing tourists, the landlady had told him. It was all one room, except for a bathroom only large enough to hold a toilet and a claw foot tub. The place was furnished in hand-me-downs so old they were now antiques. Nothing matched, giving the place a casual feel. The walls were pale brown wood paneling and the floor hardwood, except for the bathroom, which had old linoleum.

There were four rather large windows, one in the kitchen area, two in what would be a living room, but he'd moved things around so it functioned as his studio. Another window was in the bedroom, which he'd curtained off with thin cotton bedspreads he'd found at a second hand store, but they'd obviously been made in India.

The furniture consisted of a kitchen table and two chairs, an easy chair and his bed. Dylan had brought in a short set of drawers, the sawhorses and door which gave him a large table to work on. And his easel of course. And because power outages happened now and again, there was a wood stove, which Dylan had never used. Water Fae rarely got that cold, although his human body did, on occasion.

In the kitchen he drank a large glass of water. Refilling himself, from all the sweat he'd lost. Dylan glanced at the clock.

Amelia would be here in about fifteen minutes.

He shaved with a straight razor, washed and dried his face. Then changed into clean pants and a new T-shirt. He tossed his dirty clothes in the tiny laundry room and shut the door.

Her rental car drove up and parked in his empty driveway.

He went to the door.

"Good afternoon," she said. Her gray eyes gleamed, matching her long silver hair. She wore her sleek big city clothes. White pants and blazer, with a black shirt beneath. And high heels. Always high heels. And a large silver pendant with a sizable black pearl gleaming from the center of it.

"Welcome," he said.

"How's my favorite artist?" she asked, hugging him.

"I'm well. Do you have time for some tea?"

"I'd love some. Green if you have it."

He nodded and started the tea kettle. Put green tea in a teapot and pulled out two clean cups from the wooden cupboards.

"I do love this cozy little place," she said. "It suits you."

"Thanks. I love it too. How was your flight?"

"I slept through it, so that was good. I had a lot of sleep to catch up on. Too many gallery openings lately."

"I've laid out the most recent paintings. And there are stacks of others for you to look at," he said, pointing to the studio area of the cottage.

She walked over to the long table. He knew she'd been making polite small talk. What she really wanted to see were the paintings.

"Oh, this one's lovely. And I like this one too. Oh my god. I must take this one. It's extraordinary."

He looked at it. Ah. One of the underwater scenes. He wasn't sure how those would go over, but he loved them.

She continued going through the paintings as he made tea. Dylan poured the boiling water into the tea pot and inhaled the steaming leaves. Smelling their greenness. He loved feeling the heat from the steam enter his nose, carrying moisture and heat.

The tea steeped and he poured it into the mugs. He carried one over to her and she took it.

"You've outdone yourself this time. I'll certainly be able to sell these."

"Good," he said.

"I really like this one," she said. "Do you have any more along this vein?"

She was talking about the underwater scene.

He walked over to the short chest of drawers he'd bought from one of the local antique shops. It was made for holding maps and had long wide drawers which were shallow.

He opened the second drawer and pulled out about thirty paintings.

"I wasn't sure if you'd like these. They're darker and murkier than what you usually take."

He laid them on the table and picked up his tea to sip.

"Oh my god. These are amazing."

"They're my underwater scenes."

"But you don't dive."

"No. The inspirations come from my dreams."

She went through the stack of paintings, pulling a couple aside.

"I'll take all of these," she said, about the large pile. "Can you write up some sort of description about them? I think we can sell this as an entire show. Would you be willing to come back to New York?"

"I don't fly."

"Train?"

He shook his head.

"Better get on a boat then. If I can sell this idea to a large gallery, they'll expect you to be there. Meet the art buyers."

"Do you think that's where my time is best spent? I think it's better spent painting."

"If you flew it would take you less than a week. Three days. Fly in, gallery preview. Next day gallery opening. Fly home the next day."

"Not flying." He shook his head.

"Well, let me see what I can set up. This could make your career."

"I'm not interested in a career."

"You told me that you wanted to have your art seen by as many people as possible. That's what a career is. Have you changed your mind?"

"No," he said. But there was no way he'd fly to New York. Or anywhere. He was a water creature. Being up in the air, he shuddered at the idea of it.

"Okay. Well, I'll take all of these underwater ones. My goodness that's a lot."

She unzipped her large leather portfolio and lay the paintings inside, wrapping them with a soft gauzy fabric. Then she zipped it back up.

There were only two paintings she'd passed on. He'd sell those in a local store who took his work.

"Anything else you haven't shown me?"

"No. You've seen everything. Except for one that I won't part with."

"Can I see it?"

28

He nodded and pulled back one of the curtains to his bedroom. On the wall hung a painting that he'd framed with pieces of driftwood, one inch thick boards he'd found. Battered by the sea.

It had a dark perylene green base. Underwater. In the River Liffey. Where he was born thousands of years ago.

He looked at Amelia. She stood staring at the painting, her mouth open. She spoke not a word for at least five minutes. He'd never seen that reaction from her.

The painting showed undines and water sprites beneath the current. Playing, sleeping, communicating with fish, otters and diving birds, weaving water plants. The life of water spirits as he remembered it.

He longed for the family he left behind hundreds of years ago. As Faerie retreated farther from this world. And he could no longer turn a blind eye to what humans were doing to the Earth. To his beloved waterways.

Finally, Amelia said, "This. This is what I've been looking for. Forever. It's as if you're channeling E.R. Hughes. Except underwater. Can you do more of these?"

"Possibly," he said.

This painting had taken much, much longer than any of the others. Layer after layer of color. It had been difficult to get the lighting the way he saw it in his head. To show the glow which happens underwater when the sun hits the surface of the river just right.

"I understand why you don't want to sell this. I could look at it forever. All the complexity, all the beings. You know there's a huge market for fairies."

"I know."

"It's a different market than for your other work. Not fine arts. But more people love this. You would have to decide which direction you'd like your work to go. I'm not sure the market will let you do both. The people who love this wouldn't care. But the gallery people, they wouldn't touch your other work, if this got popular notice."

He nodded. He'd been aware of that.

"But with this, you could branch out into prints, cards, calendars, journals, anything. You would reach more people this way."

He knew that as well. But the people who liked "fairies" as she called them, didn't believe they were real. Or if they did, they didn't make the connection between them and the natural world which was being destroyed. They didn't necessarily have the power to stop the destruction. Which was what he wanted.

"I'll think about it," he said.

"You should think seriously about it. You're a wonderful artist. People love your work. It's hard to say this, but I'm not sure you have a right to keep your art from other people. Where would we be if Rembrandt or Degas or any of the others had kept their work private? Unseen?"

"It's not a decision I'm going to make today," he said.

"Okay. But I'm going to push you to make a decision. And I want you to paint more along this line. It's exquisite. I love your other work, but this, this is … breathtaking."

She finished packing up and left soon after that.

Dylan unpacked his paints and cleaned his brushes with a mild shampoo. Then he left them out to dry.

He was done painting for the day. The day was almost over.

He felt unsettled after showing Amelia the painting. He probably shouldn't have. Should have kept it hidden. He wasn't sure if he wanted to paint any more of these. Wasn't sure if seeing it every day was even good for him.

The old days were dead.

They'd never come again.

And the pain of losing paradise hurt him, cut him deeply. With every breath.

He needed to swim. To leave this human body behind.

At dusk, he left his human body in bed. And slunk down back alleys and side streets.

His Fae self was leaner, blended in with the landscape. The skin was a pale greenish color which like all sprites, leaked water continuously. His long stringy, green hair reached his hips. Underwater it always looked like a water plant. It took on a life of its own. His eyes saw better in the darkness. It was always a bit darker beneath the surface.

There were a few people still on the beach, farther down on the sand. He kept close to one of the tall cliffs. The rocks were sharp, but his feet were tough, even the webbed bits.

He slid into the water, loving the feel of its cool saltiness, enjoying the surf. Still, even here there was a bit of melancholy. He missed the clean swiftness of the upper Liffey. The oceans were always confused about which direction they wanted to flow. A river generally knew what it wanted. At least until it got to the ocean. Then they often flowed upstream with the high tides.

He swam beneath the surface for a long while. Reveling in breathing water in and out, cleansing himself. He hadn't allowed himself to do that in so long. He wasn't going anyplace in particular. Just swimming. The waning half moon rose in a mostly cloudless sky. It shone down beneath the waves.

After a time Dylan caught the scent of fear from an angel shark. It streaked past him. Followed by a pod of orca. Equally terrified. He turned and swam after them. Trying to discern what they were afraid of.

If they were afraid, so should he be.

He swam as fast as he could, feeling something coming up behind him. Not large, but the threat was dark. Evil.

He couldn't catch the orca or the shark. He wasn't that strong a swimmer. And he was out of shape. He headed for land.

Dylan gasped for breath.

Felt himself overtaken.

Wrapped in cold darkness.

Colder than even he could stand.

31

Frozen.
Filled with fear.
He stopped. Paralyzed.
And was taken.

Chapter 3 ⬤ Egan

Egan stood in the bustling kitchen, the calm at the center of a storm. He wiped his hands on the green apron covering his jeans and red T-shirt. A red bandana held back his black hair.

This was his world.

He loved the kitchen best of all. The chartreuse walls, the color of unripe peppers, contrasting with the steel counters and equipment. The floors were made of concrete, painted red to match many of the chiles used in the cafe. And covered with black mats at work stations to ease the workers' feet.

A driving beat played over the kitchen sound system, keeping everyone moving and on task. A good kitchen worked like a dance. Everyone doing what they were supposed to, where they were supposed to. Balancing, juggling and adapting to the circumstances.

The spicy tomato soup smelled just right. He took a

spoon and tasted the green chili sauce, set two more chilies down in front of Andre and motioned for him to add them to the sauce. Heat filled his mouth and throat, but not enough. This batch of peppers wasn't as hot as usual. The weather had been unsettled when they were ripening. Not hot and dry enough. Hopefully, the next shipment would be better.

He watched the new dishwasher. The boy kept putting dishes into the racks which still had large chunks of food on them. Then he put a plate in letting the silverware drop into the bottom of the washer.

Egan walked across the kitchen to Kevin, the head chef, and said, "You need to retrain the new boy. Now. Before he breaks the dishwasher."

Kevin nodded, watched the boy for a few minutes and went over to talk to him.

Egan made a walk through of the kitchen, checking the plates that were going out. Making adjustments to a few of them. Checking temperatures of the roasted chickens coming out of the oven.

This was what he lived for. This ballet of staff and food. The smells, the tastes combined to form an alchemy of sensation. They worked towards a common goal.

To give their customers the best possible dining experience. To connect them with their senses and with the natural world.

He left the kitchen and entered the inside dining room. It was half full. Not bad for a Santa Fe First Friday before eight P.M. Things would heat up after that, as the art patrons wandered over from the galleries. By ten the place would be packed.

Afro-Latin Jazz played softly over the sound system. Loud enough to cut the silence of the large, airy room and mask clattering dishes, soft enough to have a conversation over.

He was struck once again with how the terra cotta floor looked perfect with the eggplant colored walls. The designer had been right. Tropical vines with orange flowers grew on metal trellises attached to the walls giving impressions of abundance and lushness. The lighting was dim and romantic, candles glowed on each table. Everything was set up, white plates, chartreuse linen napkins.

The bartender was flirting madly with one of the men sitting at the bar. Perhaps a bit too much. He'd check back again later. Perhaps she needed talking to. He'd ask Maria, one of the waitresses, who never missed anything.

Egan walked outside. He stood in front of one of the patio heaters, savoring the warmth it put out. Even though the temperature outside was still in the high 60's. The warmest it had been so far this spring. He loved the heat. It was his element.

The outdoor dining room was already full. People basking in the twinkle lights and the beginning of the warm temperatures for the year.

The outside was enclosed by adobe walls, also lined with metal trellises and vines. A dark purple awning, which could easily be rolled up depending on weather conditions, covered the entire patio.

Tonight was the first night they'd opened up the outside room. It had been a mess after winter. It had taken a full week to get storm debris cleaned up, get everything hosed down and furniture moved out.

He'd hired out the planting of the pots to a local garden store. They'd done a beautiful job, the patio was now filled with large, lush tropical plants with red, yellow and orange flowers. Some of the foliage was dark purple which made a nice contrast.

Since it was still a bit chilly out, he'd need to keep a couple of the patio heaters going all night for the plants until the nighttime temperatures warmed up.

The cafe was nearly perfect. Everything running as it should.

He looked at the people next. Wait staff seemed to be doing their job. The customers looked happy. They were eating and laughing.

Everything was as it should be.

So why did he feel anxious? Something felt wrong. Not just a little off. Completely wrong.

He needed to be himself to understand. To let go of this human body and be who he was. Perhaps later tonight. After the rush.

He pulled the phone from his jeans pocket and texted Tomas. *Can I make glass tonight?*

Then Egan went back inside and stood in the shadows, looking at customers and watching the bartender. She was definitely flirting too much. Getting her job done, but too much flirting.

His phone pinged back.

Sure. I'll be leaving at 10. Let yourself in and make sure you lock up and shut everything down when you go. I'll leave the furnaces on.

Egan smiled.

Hopefully, in the heat he'd be able to figure out what was wrong.

He glanced at the filling tables again. He recognized Samuel Fredrickson, a local reviewer. Well, it had to happen. Good to know he was in the house.

Egan stepped back into the kitchen.

"Okay, look lively people. We've got a reviewer up front. Let's focus and do better than our best, okay?"

"Sure boss," said Kevin.

His reply was echoed by the rest of the kitchen staff.

They were a good bunch, his crew. Dependable, skilled and hard working. A few of them even had the gift of genius.

Once a week, he and Kevin let each of the line cooks design a special menu item. That kept them excited and creative. A sort of competition had grown up between them, each trying to come up with something that would blow the others out of the water. They were each other's competition, as well as biggest fans.

The night moved quickly with nothing going wrong other than little things. The dishwasher, a homeless kid, would work out. Eventually.

The bartender was another matter. Egan talked with her on her break and found she was slurring her words. He smelled her soda glass and it reeked with whisky. He fired her on the spot, giving her two weeks of extra pay and making her promise to get help. He called in another bartender and staffed the bar until she arrived.

Egan wasn't a great bartender. Didn't have the gift of chitchat.

After closing, he shut down the immaculate kitchen, turned off all but two of the outdoor heaters, set the alarm system and took the deposit to the bank. There wasn't that much. Most people paid with cards these days. Still, he didn't want it sitting around the cafe.

He walked from the bank to Tomas' shop. It was becoming chilly, might even get below freezing tonight. He was wrapped up in a warm wool jacket and wore gloves.

The streets were still busy with people going to the few galleries still open or to late night cafes or bars. He went down the alley and frightened a cat away from its kill. Probably a rat. He didn't look.

He unlocked Tomas' door and went in, locking it behind him. He punched in the code for the security system, then reset it.

It was deliciously warm in the front room. He walked through the showroom, filled with glorious glass art in vibrant colors and fluid shapes, lit only by a few strands of dim lights.

In the back, he turned lights on, shutting the door to the front room. He didn't want customers seeing the light and knocking on the door.

He didn't want to be disturbed.

The back room was all concrete. Gray and boring. Egan had a hard time understanding why Tomas had such a beautiful shop, but kept his workspace so ugly. Maybe it inspired him to make such beautiful art.

The furnaces were running just fine. Egan took off his coat and gloves. He sat in an old wood chair close to the supplies, out of the main work area. Then he slid out of his human body. It slumped back in the chair, looking dead.

Egan gazed back at it. Leaving it behind always made him feel sort of melancholy.

His Fae body was humanoid, but hairless. His head, back and the tops of his arms were scaled in reds, oranges and yellows. As he'd aged, a bit of black had appeared. His skin had an orange tinge to it.

He opened the largest furnace and crept inside. The opening was barely large enough to get his shoulders through and his body felt cramped. His lizard-like scales sucked in the heat coming from a heating element above. He pulled the door closed as much as he could from the inside and crouched in the heat. The surface of the furnace felt like rough concrete, although it was probably some sort of synthetic stone mixture. He closed his eyes, pretending the heat was actual flames.

Someday, he'd buy a house way out in the country and build massive fires every night. And bask in their heat.

Of course it wasn't the same as it used to be. There used to be others. But they'd all retreated with the rest of Faerie. He hadn't been able to let go of the world. He was older than most Fae. Had been alive since before the Earth cooled.

He'd lived inside volcanoes most recently. Loved the sulfurous fumes.

He loved the human world and he missed Faerie.

There was no way he could have both.

He went deeper inside himself.

What was this danger he'd been feeling? It felt menacing. Dark and cold.

He sensed confinement, restriction.

Pain.

He felt incredible pain.

His limbs were frozen and he gasped in agony.

It was real.

He pulled himself back to reality.

He couldn't move.

Egan found himself in a cold iron box.

Which was moving.

Every part of him was in torment.

What was happening?

He had no answers and finally his consciousness fled.

Chapter 4 ❦ Adaire

Adaire glanced at the cloud filled sky. It felt like rain. Moisture gathered in the air, making it heavy. The street was nearly empty of traffic, since it was midday. But it was lined with parked cars.

It must be nearly one. She hadn't happily adopted the human concept of time, but she was trying to keep appointments.

The planting strip was anchored with grand horse chestnut trees. They were all in bloom. This variety had coral pink flowers held upright on panicles larger than her head. The trees were glorious. They had a faint sweet scent that no human could ever smell.

She turned the corner onto a side street and was astonished to find a large front garden almost completely filled with Rhodies. All in bloom at once. At least it was a stunning show.

Adaire didn't want to think about what it would look like in a couple of months. She believed in diversity. Nature planted that way. Humans should too.

Two more blocks.

She tugged at her black hoodie and glanced down at her khaki pants and work boots. Her long black hair tied back. She looked like a Gardening Coach. Professional. Like she knew her stuff.

Which she did.

She was a dryad in a human's body. She understood plants at a level humans never could. She understood the soil and how it affected plants. And while masquerading as a human, she'd taught herself about their view of plants.

Humans understood so little.

She walked past gardens with scraggly unkempt foliage and a stray tulip or late daffodil cropping up. Other yards were completely barren, nothing but overgrown grass. Some front yards were completely filled with concrete.

Those made her weep inwardly. Better to have covered it with gravel and beautiful rocks.

Adaire kept going until she reached the address on her post-it note.

The house was a Craftsman style built on a rare double lot. Rare for this part of the city at least. It looked like the dwelling had recently been repainted and shined up.

The garden needed a lot of work.

A hundred foot tall Douglas fir, which was struggling, had been planted far too close to the house and was awkwardly pruned off on the side next to the building. In the back yard stood a towering blue spruce which was brown and nearly bare, probably from spruce aphids.

When would people in Seattle stop trying to grow blue spruce? The trees just weren't meant to grow in the maritime Northwest.

The garden was absolutely overgrown. Too many big shrubs in too small a space. None of them had enough room. They weren't happy. The front garden was shaded by the fir and filled with fungal diseases. There was no air flow.

She had no problems with funguses, but most humans

wanted nice looking gardens with healthy plants. This one didn't qualify.

Would the back be worse or better? And how could she politely tell this woman her garden was a disaster?

Adaire climbed the steps and knocked on the door.

A pale woman with short blond hair answered. She was older, perhaps in her 50's.

"Are you Eleni?" asked Adaire.

"Yes. Adaire?"

Adaire nodded.

"Oh, do come in. I need to get my shoes."

Adaire went inside the entry way and stood in an area where shoes were stacked neatly.

Eleni sat on the bottom step of stairs which led to the second story. She tied a pair of running shoes.

"Would you like a cup of tea?" she asked.

"No thank you. I just finished some before I left home," said Adaire.

She looked into the living room. Hardwood floors, Mission style, brown leather furniture and white walls with framed Impressionistic prints on them. The house looked immaculate and spare. Everything in its place. A mixture of hardness and softness.

"Okay, where shall we start?" asked Eleni. "Front or back?"

"Wherever you'd like," Adaire said.

"Let's begin in front. Oh, I have so many questions. Thank you for coming."

"You're welcome."

Adaire followed her out the front door, closing it behind them. They walked down the concrete steps and stood on the front sidewalk.

Eleni said, "I just bought the house a month ago. I've always lived in apartments. So, I'm brand new at this. I just retired and I want to learn how to garden."

"Do you know what sort of garden you want?"

She noticed Eleni had a clipboard with a pen stuck onto the clasp.

"I've been tearing pages out of magazines. I thought you could tell me what's possible and what's not."

Eleni turned the pages of blank paper back until she came to glossy magazine photos. Then she handed the clipboard to Adaire.

Adaire looked through the pages of photos pulled from the pages of garden magazines. Exquisite gardens each of them, or they wouldn't have been chosen for publication. Each one had a balance of evergreens and deciduous, perennial and annual, trees and shrubs. There was beautiful hardscaping and skilled stonework. Lovely garden art and beautiful water features.

"These are all very ambitious gardens," she said, looking at Eleni.

"But could I do them?"

"They require substantial money, unless you're planning on doing the paths and fencing yourself. As far as the actual gardening, yes you could do that. It's a matter of choosing the right plants for your space, but this sort of garden is extremely time consuming. All-consuming."

"I just retired. The house is perfect. I have no family. I'll go mad unless I have an all consuming thing to do."

"Okay then. The only problem I have with nearly all the gardens you've chosen is that they're full sun gardens. You've got that massive tree there that throws your front garden in complete shade. I'm guessing the spruce in the back yard does the same. It looks like it's on the south side of your lot."

Eleni motioned for Adaire to follow her. She opened the warped gate made of old wire fencing and they went into the back.

It was worse than the front. Rose bushes, stringy and covered with disease languished in the shade. A stray daffodil here and there managed to live with the shade. Mostly, it was buttercups and blackberry vines. No one had touched this garden in years.

"Same problem back here," said Adaire. "This was once a lovely full sun garden. Now, it's all in shade. The spruce that's making the shade here, plus the fir that's out front, are both sick trees."

"Can they be saved?" Eleni asked.

"The spruce isn't suited to our climate. It's got spruce aphids. It would take tons of chemicals to keep it alive. And it will never regrow the parts that are brown or bare. The fir out front, I'm not sure what's wrong with it. You could call in an arborist, who could probably tell you one way or another."

Adaire hated to pronounce judgement on a tree. She was a dryad after all. These were her kin. But both trees were suffering. The spruce it would be kinder to let die. The fir, she wasn't sure. In this human body her senses were dulled. She couldn't sense everything. Human bodies were so limited.

"If this were your garden, what would you do?"

"I would remove both trees, and I'd find out why the fir is dying. Make sure it's not a soil problem. Then I'd put in the hardscaping. Paths and fences. A patio if you want one. Then I'd enrich the soil everywhere. It looks drained. I'd remove all the invasive weeds and probably a few other shrubs. Give the ones you want to keep more space. And everything I can see here needs a good pruning. Except perhaps that Hamamelis, the witch hazel there. Give the garden more light and airflow."

"I agree with you. I feel bad about cutting down mature trees, but both of them look terrible."

"You can always plant more trees. Do some research. Plant trees that are the right size for your garden. Choose shorter trees and plant them on the north side of your garden so they work as a winter wind break and don't fill your garden with shade. You have so many choices here."

Eleni was scribbling down things on her clipboard as fast as Adaire said them.

The consultation continued. Adaire identified the different shrubs and Eleni took more notes. They went over Eleni's plans she'd drawn up for the garden and Adaire helped her decide what was workable.

Adaire left her a long list of resources for which Eleni was grateful. They agreed that Eleni would make another appointment once the trees were down, wooden fencing was up and paths were done. Then Eleni would have compost delivered and start shoveling it onto all the beds. Eleni was going to have her compost bins built, so making compost and pruning would be the first lesson.

Adaire waved goodbye and began the walk back to the daylight basement she rented from the homeowner. Her senses felt duller than usual.

She needed to get out into the woods.

Alone.

Her friend Max was out of town. He liked to go camping out in the woods and stay up all night taking photos of the sky and use his telescope.

She'd have to settle for the Arboretum.

That night she left her human body in the bed of her small apartment in the basement. As she went out to the street. Adaire made herself gossamer, then invisible. She climbed on the back of a jeep, that had a tire mounting to hold onto, her feet on the bumper. Trying not to breathe in the awful exhaust and ignoring the jangling sensation the car gave her from its motor. She hated cars.

Some Fae weren't bothered by a lot of the metals, she was.

Adaire rode it all the way to the University District. Then she ran across the University Bridge. Keeping to the shadows, just in case someone, or something could penetrate her invisibility.

She caught the back of a small pickup and rode it

over to Montlake. She walked the remaining blocks to the Arboretum.

Fluidly slipping through the wrought iron fence, she was in the forest. A highly cultivated forest, but there were many big trees, all the same. Tonight she moved towards the oaks. She needed their strength.

Adaire climbed up into the largest one just as Security came by. Once the guard left, she was alone. Just her, the trees, the sleeping squirrels. And birds, some awake, some not. And a few insects.

Her senses expanded outwards. Taking pleasure in the feeling of sap rising in the oaks. She could almost taste their green juiciness. They'd just begun to leaf out and all their energy was moving towards upward growth.

It was been too long since she'd been one with a tree.

Her cheek rubbed against the rough bark, the scent of rain in the air. She felt blissful, here in the green forest. Even if it was human made and highly managed. The trees were strong and alive and she reveled in their power.

Why had she left all this behind to live in the human world? This was where she belonged.

Her brothers and sisters had retreated to the trees. Chosen not to take part in the human world. Chosen to let it take them when their trees were cut down, killing them as well.

Chosen suicide rather than positive action.

Why didn't she just choose a nice tree and live in it?

She was lost in the juiciness of the tree when the warning came.

Her senses yelled, "Flee!"

A suction was pulling her from the tree, like a giant vacuum.

She screamed. Tried to hang tight to the oak's branches.

But the wrenching was too strong.

Her hands slipped. She was thrown into a large metal box. The lid closed. It felt like agony.

The metal burned her.
Her soul felt torn.
Then she lost consciousness.
Weeping for the loss of the tree. And the pain.

Chapter 5 ✦ Skye

Skye was kept in the small box for hours. She tried not to touch it, but it was so small, she couldn't expand her wings. She had to sit on the bottom and be curled up in a fetal position so she wasn't touching the walls or top.

The cold iron burned her. It made her brain jangled and tangled. She couldn't think straight. The pain set her teeth on edge. Her mouth felt dry and she needed water.

She could feel the box being jostled around as if it was being moved.

Her mind raced. Who would want to do this to her? Entrap her?

She had no answers.

The burning sensation made her stay in her mind. She tried not to acknowledge her body. The pain was unbearable.

So, she kept thinking. Planning a way out.

Eventually, the small box was opened at the bottom and she was dumped in a cell. The floor was concrete and she hit it hard, unable to get her wings open in time. She tried to fly up out the still open top, but the lid of cold iron was dropped too quickly for her and she hit that hard too.

Skye was slapped back to the floor by the lid, but this time she landed on her feet.

The cell she was in was just a larger box. About ten feet square and tall. She fluttered her wings anxiously. It was dimly lit by her own glow.

The sides were hard metal of some kind, imbedded with bars of cold iron. She kept away from them, staying in the center of the room. The cold iron made her uncomfortable. She'd built up a small amount of tolerance for human metals, depending on the components. Cold iron was the worst.

She paced in a circle in the center of the box. For what must have been hours and hours. This box didn't move. She'd been dumped here. By someone who knew she'd be affected by the cold iron.

Who and why?

It wasn't as debilitating as the small box which had been solid cold metal, but it was bad enough.

Eventually, she lay down and napped lightly.

When she woke, the same things rolled around in her head. Whoever had caught her had known her. Had been watching her and waiting for her to fly.

She felt thirsty and moved her thick, dry tongue around inside her mouth, trying to get some saliva flowing. She fluttered her wings half-heartedly and folded them neatly behind her.

Skye sat up. Her arms around her knees. Remembering the history of the Fae. Had things really happened the way she'd been taught?

Or had their history happened just like the humans? Written and rewritten by those who'd won. Those who were currently in power. Those who'd retreated from the world, back into Faerie.

After a long time, the ceiling opened in one corner and a body dropped into the room with her.

It landed on the concrete with a hard thud.

Chapter 6 ☙ Egan

Egan opened his eyes. He lay on a concrete floor inside a cold iron cage. It was dimly lit and he was freezing. He sensed heat in one area.

Then he saw her. A sylph, sitting on the floor, knees pulled up to her chest and arms wrapped around her knees. She had a far away look on her face. As if she was trying to shut out everything.

He could smell nothing except the metal. His mouth was dry and his belly grumbling. How long had he been out?

His shoulder ached. He must have landed on it the wrong way. He rolled it around, trying to loosen the muscles.

He sat up and she opened her eyes, stared at him with unseeing eyes. He could tell her mind was elsewhere.

The amount of pain he saw in her eyes made him gasp.

He shivered from the cold.

She saw him, recognized his problem and came to him, huddling up next to him. To share her warmth. She felt terribly overheated for a sylph. Feverish.

"Where are we?" he asked.

"I don't know. I was plucked from the skies over the Olympic Mountains. In Washington state. You?"

"I was taken from a furnace in Santa Fe."

She shrugged.

"Have you seen anyone?"

She shook her head.

"So we don't know what they want."

"No," she said, softly. She buried her head in her arms.

He felt the gossamer softness of her wings against his scales. He'd never had much to do with sylphs or any of the flying folk really. They'd almost lived in different worlds, different habitats, even though they were both Fae.

Sylphs were the beautiful ones of Faerie. Slender and tall, with beautiful wings and silky hair down to their ankles. They had blue eyes the color of a summer sky. And often bluish tinged skin. He had never seen a sylph, male or female, who wasn't stunning.

Fire Fae, like him were often considered unattractive. They were sometimes tall and slender like him, but just as often, short, squat and stocky. Covered in yellow, orange, red and sometimes black scales on their backs, shoulders, the tops of their arms and often on the back, sides and top of their heads. Where other Fae had long, luscious hair, fire Fae were hairless. Hair would burn in the fires.

His sharp ears caught a grating sound. From above. He looked up and saw the ceiling sliding. A small space opened and a dark shape was dropped inside.

It landed on the concrete. And lay there motionless. A water sprite.

Then the ceiling snapped back into place as if it was a large box.

If he'd been able, perhaps he could have jumped out through the hole. But he was too cold, sluggish. His muscles wouldn't work well enough. He'd risk touching the cold iron in the walls.

The thought of that agony kept him from moving. Normally, he could've touched the wall, if he hadn't been so cold. The cold made him weak.

So Egan sat and watched the sprite lying there. He could sense its life, the cold wetness of it.

The sylph also just sat there, lost in her pain and fear. She would be no help in coming up with a plan for escape.

Finally, the sprite came to consciousness. He sat up in one fluid motion and looked around. He saw Egan looking at him and nodded.

Egan returned the nod.

The water sprite was greenish, like most, with stringy, grasslike hair and slightly webbed feet and hands. He looked a little doughy, but Egan knew that was an illusion. Water sprites were massively strong.

The sprite sat looking around, taking everything in, but saying nothing.

Egan ran through the possibilities of why they had been captured, but nothing stayed. None of this made sense.

What seemed like hours later, the ceiling cracked open in another place and dropped another body. This one was conscious. It landed on its feet with a great thud.

It was a she. A dryad. Her eyes burned with anger.

She stood in the corner where she'd been dropped. Looked around and saw all of them.

Dryads were known for their height and slenderness. She also had greenish tinged skin and knee-length black hair. An angular body, that looked slight, but he knew she was strong.

He'd wrestled with a dryad once. Only once.

"What are we doing here?" she asked, her eyes nearly flaming. Impressive for a dryad.

"I don't know," said Egan.

"Where are we? What's happening?" she asked.

"It's obvious, isn't it?" said the sylph next to him.

"No," said the dryad.

"Someone's hunting Fae who live with humans," the sylph said.

"Why? And how? And who?" asked the water sprite.

The sylph shrugged.

"I'm Egan," he said.

"Dylan," said the sprite.

"Skye," said the sylph.

"Adaire," said the dryad.

"Why are we here?" asked Adaire again.

"Could it be whoever's the Luminary in Faerie these days?" asked Skye.

"Perhaps. Or someone who wants to break Faerie," said Adaire, walking over and sitting next to Egan and Skye.

Dylan got up and joined them. Sitting down with a squishy sound, water dripped off his slippery looking skin.

"Why do you say that?" Dylan asked.

"Well, we're all here aren't we?" Adaire said. "Air," she pointed at Skye "Fire," she pointed at him. "Water," she pointed at Dylan. "Earth," she pointed at herself.

"You need more than the four elements to break Faerie," said Dylan.

"What else do you need?" asked Egan. He didn't think it was possible to bring down the boundary Faerie had put up. Only from within and by the ones who made the enclosure in the first place.

"A vast amount of power, I'd guess," said Adaire

"You're full of power," said Dylan.

"Why else would someone abduct us? You were abducted weren't you?"

"Yes, I was," said Dylan. "There are plenty of reasons

why someone would do this. I prefer not to speculate about it at the moment."

"What?" asked Egan.

Dylan held out his webbed hand and began counting off on his fingers as he spoke, "We're a zoo. Captured Fae. We're entertainment. Twisted or not. They want our power. Want to use us to gain power in the human world. I could go on, but I don't want to venture there."

The room fell silent then.

They waited for hours.

No more Fae were dropped into the cell.

He hoped there weren't more cells of trapped Fae in this place.

No water was offered. They all suffered from the nearness of the cold iron. Egan hoped they'd be able to escape.

All he had right now was hope.

Egan went deep inside himself and found the warmth. The heat. And basked in it. Feeling it spread throughout his body.

Keeping himself alive.

Chapter 7 ✦ Balor

Balor sat bent over in the darkness, elbows braced on his knees and both normal eyes closed. His third eye, in the middle of his forehead and bald head, was covered with seven colored bandanas. Yellow, orange, red, purple, blue, green and black on the top layer. He was a giant, perched on the stout metal stool sitting in the middle of the nearly empty, dilapidated warehouse.

He could smell the decades of filth that had piled up in the building. Human garbage. Mouse droppings. Woodsmoke from his fire drifted past his nose. Birds nested up near the ceiling, the tiny cries of their young breaking the silence.

The old warehouse was made of rusted metal pieces, many of them torn off and blown away over time. Broken windows let the wind blow through the ruins, making his aged gray pants and shirt feel thin.

The same wind which told him the others would come.

He felt sure of it.

He'd sent out the call.

They would take back their world, once again.

The Fae would be defeated. Once and for all.

His mouth felt gritty from the blowing sand. He'd brought the drought here with him. And as long as he stayed, so would the drought. Even with his third eye covered.

He spat.

The Fae had stolen his lands, conquered his people by war and interbreeding, finally exiling them. Now the new gods had suffered the same conquest by humans. The Fae were weak.

Faerie, having closed itself, existed in the same space as the human world, but humans couldn't reach Faerie now.

It was as if Faerie had covered the land and the sky with a huge invisible and magical cloth. Passing through that cloth would take one to Faerie, although only Fae could pass through. Walking on the land would take one to the same physical space on Earth that the humans now held, except there would be no sign of Faerie, even though it was there.

Balor meant to see that cloth removed and all of Faerie destroyed. All Fae murdered. Then that space of Earth would belong to the Fomorians again.

He spat at the fire, hearing the spittle sizzle as it dried out. Such would be his drought. He would make Faerie pay. He'd devastate their land.

They thought the old gods, the first gods, the Fomorians were dead.

Gone.

But the Fomorians had only hidden, tucked themselves away over the wide world. Waiting for the right time. Like the Fae were doing, hunkered down in Faerie. Except for the few stragglers.

All of whom Balor had captured.

Easily.

The Fae were weak and stupid. They'd grown soft living among humans. They were no longer warriors.

First the Fomorians would exterminate the Fae, just like all of Faerie had tried to do to them.

Only he, Balor, would make sure the Fomorians succeeded.

Then, it would be a simple thing to enslave the humans. They had no magical powers and their 'technology', the god they worshipped, would be easily defeated.

He threw more wood on the fire and watched the flames take hold.

Famine, drought, storms, winds, the strength of the seas, earthquakes, all those and more were the tools he and his people had at their disposal.

This time they would win.

Chapter 8 ⟡ Fiachna

Fiachna walked through the knee deep grass and heather, the dew on the plants wetting his deerskin pants to up to the knees. The heather was blooming in white, purple and pink. A heron flew past him so close that Fiachna could feel the wind created from its wings. The world smelled fresh and new.

Spring was here, after the long darkness of winter.

The birds were nesting. New plants poking up through the soil. Trees beginning to bud out again.

So why did he feel so old and tired? So alone?

He adjusted his brown cloak, worn thin from centuries of use.

He followed the old dirt trail up to the mound, sensing something wrong.

As he came closer he saw darkness.

The burial mound had been opened.

Stones closing the entryway bashed into pieces. He stepped inside and in the darkness he could see the grave had been violated. Bones strewn around in a display of arrogance.

Whatever had done this had no respect for the dead.

The smell that lingered wasn't from anything he'd ever smelled before. The intruder hadn't been human. Or animal.

It was something else. Something that tickled his memory. But it was so long ago that he had only a vague recollection. A threatening shadowy figure.

Then even the memory was gone.

He puzzled over this. Normally, when the mounds were tampered with, it was curious humans. Sometimes malicious ones.

But never a mysterious being.

Fiachna picked up the ancient bones and arranged them as they should have been. He sang the songs of his ancestors to them, a strong melody of courage and love. He placed the scant pieces of ornamentation in their proper places.

Hours later, he used his magic to move large boulders to close the opening, sealing it with a song of the stone Fae, deep and rumbling. He placed chunks of turf over them until the mound looked undisturbed.

"Sleep again, my friend."

He secured the grave and drawing strength from the land around him, Fiachna tied the mound back into the boundary of Faerie. The graves all anchored the boundaries.

"We are built upon the bones of the past."

This would need to be reported.

He called and a raven flew up and landed on his outstretched arm.

"Hello my friend. You must go to the Luminary. You must tell him I have found a disturbed grave mound. It was not disturbed by human or Fae. It was something else, much older. He must know this."

The raven made a gurgling sound and flew off to deliver the message.

The day was mostly over, and although he was exhausted, Fiachna continued on with his never ending work.

Checking the boundaries.

There was no one else.

Chapter 9 ⚬ Adaire

Adaire stared at Dylan. He was curled into a fetal position on the cold concrete floor, dark circles beneath his eyes. His skin had stopped weeping water. It looked shriveled, as if there was no more water to give.

The cold iron affected him and Skye the most.

Skye sat cross-legged, eyes flashing around, looking for a way out. She made small whimpering sounds. Panicked noises.

It was still dark in the cell. She had no idea how long they'd been there. No food or water had been offered. No contact with their captors at all. Or captor. She didn't even know how many there were.

She could smell the sea on Dylan. Salt and fish. Skye smelled like feathers and clean fresh wind. Egan smelled like a fire burning wet wood. Smoke.

Egan was curled into a tight ball between Adaire and Skye, trying to share their body heat. His heat burned

Adaire slightly, but she didn't move away. He seemed more affected by the cold than the iron.

Adaire was only affected a little by the cold iron. It was iron that had been forged for a very long time over relatively low temperature. Cold forged iron had an energetic presence that hindered the Fae's use of magic, and even their life. Humans didn't generally use it anymore, having discovered stronger metals and alloys, which they generally heated at higher temperatures, releasing the energy trapped within.

Adaire was at home with most minerals. The cold iron weakened her, but not like it did the others.

She could see the spaces between the molecules in the iron bars.

Could she make them move?

Adaire let her energy wander over towards the wall. She gently explored the structure of the cold iron bars and the steel panels. She let her energy play with the molecules and atoms, trying to make the spaces larger in just one small area. It was difficult to tell in the darkness if anything changed.

Through the small holes she could feel life. Others. There were other Fae in the cell next to theirs. She could feel earth and water. No fire or air.

She shifted her body and turned to another wall. Shifting things around gently, not pushing. She'd save that for later.

On the other side of that wall, she felt no life. It was an empty cell. Death lingered in that cell. Its occupants had

been killed. The elements inside, the energies that had been part of the dead Fae, were depleted. They begged for release. She held the space open so they could enter her own cell. Their energy flowed into Dylan's, Skye's and Egan's bodies. There had been no earth spirit held prisoner there.

Egan sat up, watching her and the wall. The fire energy that had flowed into him had woken him. He look more alert from the infusion. Had he known the fire Fae who had died?

Skye and Dylan hadn't reacted.

She let the molecules slide back, closing the hole and turned to another wall. Beyond it was a completely empty cell. Turning to the last wall, she found what she sought. Beyond that wall lay no more cells. No more cold iron. It was the way out, provided she could move the molecules.

She let go and collapsed her energy back into herself.

Adaire staggered back to the center of the room and plopped down on the hard floor. She'd gone too far.

She pointed at the last wall and said to Egan, "Mark that wall. It's the way out."

Then she collapsed into unconsciousness.

Chapter 10 ✦ Skye

Skye came back to herself when someone else's air drifted past, seeping in through her skin. It smelled stale and was imprisoned air, but different than the air in this cell. Its presence enlivened her, strengthened her waning energy.

She wrapped her power around the foreign air, comforting it. Mourning its loss of the original Fae who hosted the energy. Where had the air element come from? It wasn't exactly someone else's soul, but it was close. And it was ancient and powerful.

Skye sat up and looked around, her vision clear in the near darkness. The iron cell hadn't changed.

The others were awake, except for Adaire. She seemed diminished.

Egan burned brightly, he stood next to one of the walls. She watched as he shot fire at the wall, burning a spiral deeply into it. The metal glowed from his heat. Skye watched with awe as he melted a layer of the metal wall and heated up one of the iron bars. The smell of burnt metal filled the cell.

Then he moved back to them and plopped down next to Skye. She knew he was conserving his strength. She blew at him, fanning his flames a bit, sharing strength.

He smiled.

Dylan sat alert, on the cold concrete floor. He looked newly invigorated as well, reeking of salt and kelp.

"What happened to Adaire?" asked Skye.

"She moved the wall, I saw it," said Egan.

He pointed, "In that room are two earth and two water spirits. In that one, there were two fire, one water and one air. In that direction, nothing. In that," he said, gesturing to the wall he'd marked, "lies our escape."

"How?" asked Dylan.

Egan said, "If she can open it wide enough, we can slip through and leave."

"She's not strong enough," said Skye.

"And what about those others?" asked Dylan. "We all felt their presence. Can we help them escape too?"

"I don't know," said Egan. "I'm not sure if she'll have the strength to open both walls. I can help some, but she's far stronger."

"If she can open the wall between these, then perhaps the earth spirits in the cell can help her open the other," said Skye.

"It's a gamble," said Dylan. "We could weaken ourselves so much we don't have enough energy or time left to escape."

"It might take more time," said Egan

"We don't know how much time we have," said Skye.

"I think we should try," said Egan.

Dylan slid to an upright position. "You mean Adaire should try."

"Can we do anything?" asked Skye.

"You burned the wall, Egan. Perhaps I can rust it."

"Will that work?" asked Egan.

Dylan shrugged.

He moved towards the wall the two cells shared sliding like an amoebic human. It was very strange to watch. Skye noticed he didn't touch the wall. About a foot away he spurted salty water at it in just one spot.

She wasn't putting too much hope that rusting the wall would help anything. Not for decades. She knew they didn't have that much time. They would dissipate before then.

After about an hour, Dylan said, "I can hear them doing the same on the other side. Maybe when Adaire's stronger, they can help her. They must know we're here."

Skye listened and realized she'd heard them shooting water at the wall for a while. Dylan was just closer and louder.

Egan stood and went over to the wall he'd marked. He began flaming at it again. Melting more area, making the wall thinner. The cell began to get smokier. But one of the bars was completely melted through.

Skye decided to concentrate on Adaire. Letting her healing energies work on the dryad.

She knelt over her, letting her power flow into the earth Fae. Gently pulling her upward to a place where she could benefit from the healing. Bringing her back to a stable place. Helping build her energy back up.

Chapter 11 ✦ Baylor

Baylor paced around the exterior of the cold iron cells he'd made. His dark skin made him barely visible in the low light of the abandoned warehouse. No one would see him. He could feel spring returning to the land, energy beginning to flow up from the soil. Smell the fresh rain in the air. The bare trees were budding out. Male frogs had begun to croak, searching for a mate.

His stomach growled with hunger. It had been days since he'd eaten.

His mouth felt dry. He should go find some water.

But he continued pacing a circular path around the warehouse.

This would be another hungry year. There would be no planting this year. Not until his people had reclaimed their land. There would be only fighting and war.

This was good.

They had waited thousands of years for this.

He felt the fog move through and knew she was here. Cethlenn.

Wife.

Her bare feet padded on the concrete warehouse floor as she came into solid form, deftly avoiding broken bottles, cans and other rubbish.

"Husband," she said.

He held out his arms and embraced her warm body and she his. Their bodies moulded together as if they hadn't been apart for thousands of years.

He had missed her terribly.

His people had all separated in order to remain hidden. They were such powerful beings. Together they would have been too easy to track by the vile Fae.

"It has been so long," she said.

"Too long since we separated."

She nodded, looking around. "Are the others here?"

"Not yet, you are the first to arrive."

"I have spent those years traversing the edges of Faerie. Watching it shrink. Watching them withdraw from the world. Except for a few strays," she said, wearily.

"I've been spending that time collecting those strays," he said, gesturing to the iron cells.

She cocked her head and smiled. "What will you do with them?"

"I'm not sure. Some have died, weakened by the cold iron. Others may serve as leverage with the Fae. If not, we will enjoy killing them, won't we? As an example."

Cethlenn sighed deeply. "I have watched the Fae kill so many of us. I've watched them kill humans. Then humans bred faster than even mice. They've driven the Fae deep into Faerie. But humans kill themselves and everyone else. There are too many of them. I am sick of death."

"But we must retake our home," said Balor.

How could she not understand this?

"What will we do with all the humans that populate it? They've paved the land. Built huge buildings. Our land has been changed."

"Destroy their cities. Tear the buildings down. Flood the land and cleanse it of humans."

She shook her head. "I don't think that's possible. They are as tenacious as fleas."

Water sloshed around his feet and the wind picked up.

Balor said, "Corb and Conand are here."

A huge man with a hump on one shoulder and one leg longer than the other limped into the warehouse, accompanied by pools of water.

The breeze brought another man. His waist-long hair and beard blew in the wind which swirled around him. He floated in the air even as he came into solid form.

"We have come," said Conand, the North Wind.

"Good."

Corb of the sea asked, "How many will come?"

"I do not know," said Balor. "I don't know how many heard the call. I don't know how many of us are left."

"I was killed," said Conand of the wind. "But we cannot die."

"I was killed," said Balor. "But no one can kill death."

He smiled.

"Some of our blood was tainted though," said Cethlenn. "Even our own daughter mated with one of them. We lost her and her children."

Conand nodded. "It is so with many of our kind. There are few of us left."

"I represent Domnu. Mother of us all, she of the deep abyss of the oceans. She cannot come here, but will do whatever we ask. She longs for revenge," said Corb.

Balor nodded.

Domnu's presence would be more than any of them could stand. She controlled the deep oceans. It was not time to empty them. Yet. But if that's what it took to displace the Fae, he would see it done.

"Do you have a battle plan?" asked Conand.

"I have ideas. I will wait to see how many of us there are before I decide which one we shall use. But our time is here. The Fae have mostly retreated into Faerie. They have dwindled in number. They are weak. I have spent decades capturing the few who stayed out in the world. But I've finally finished. They are contained in these iron boxes. We can attack Faerie unhindered and without warning. They believe we are all dead. Fools."

Conand nodded.

"How long will you wait for the others?" asked Corb.

"We have waited thousands of years. I only called for you two days ago. We will wait two more days. In the meantime, let us find some food. I am starving," said Balor.

"Are humans any good to eat?" asked Conand.

"Too stringy," said Cethlenn. "I think we should look for sheep or cattle."

"Cattle," said Corb.

"Let's go hunting," said Cethlenn.

"I'll stay here," said Balor. "I'll call again and wait for the others."

Cethlenn, Corb and Conand went out into the night, taking the fog, wind and water with them.

Balor walked on the wet floor around the wall of iron boxes, back to his stool. He picked up a wooden pallet and tossed it onto the fire as if it were a small stick. The wind brought the smoke in his direction. He breathed it in deeply. Willing to take the fire's power and mingle it with his own.

Being a giant was easy in this world of small humans.

Chapter 12 ⚬ Dylan

Dylan stood staring at the wall of the cell. The cold iron set his teeth on edge. As well as the rest of his body. It was as if his body was screaming at him *get out of here—you're going to die otherwise*. He hated this place.

The cold iron bars were backed with steel. The cold iron was probably weaker and more vulnerable to rust.

He pulled water up from the earth below, through the concrete and onto the bars of cold iron. It was salt water. They must be near the sea. He could taste the green kelp, smell the salmon as the water flowed through his body and out the tips of his fingers.

After it hit the wall, it ran down to the floor and across the concrete back to him, his skin filtered out anything other than the water and then sucked up the water and shot it back up to his fingertips, keeping a steady flow going.

He could feel water hitting the other side of the wall with more force than his. There were two water spirits in there. Adaire hadn't been able to open the wall long enough for him to identify what type they might be: Sprites, kelpies or any of the other varieties of water guardians. Or even if he knew them.

It was enough that they were trying to help.

Eventually, he had to stop. He stood there, slightly drooped over, resting.

Otherwise his energy would lower beyond his ability to recover. Finally, he dropped down into a small pool of water still on the concrete. Taking solace in the wetness.

Vaguely, he noticed Adaire was standing. She walked over to the wall and touched it with her bare hands, which amazed him. How could she stand the iron?

He could tell she was shifting things around with the wall. Water began to seep through from the other side, then stopped. He could feel the other water spirits resting too.

The hole was large enough he could sense two earth spirits come to the wall. They were helping Adaire do whatever she was doing.

He knew the metal hadn't rusted much, but the constant water on it, for hours on end had weakened it somewhat.

Skye came up behind him and touched his shoulders. He felt her energy mingle with his. Even though she was an air spirit and couldn't normally share energy with him, she was obviously a healer. Matching his energy, she helped him recover.

He basked in her breeze and napped sitting up, dreaming of the ocean on a summer day. Dylan dreamt he heard gulls crying out as they surfed the wind. Crows dropped mussels on the rocks, trying to crack them. Shore birds with long legs walked among the tide pools looking for food. Kelp baked in the sun, perfuming the air.

When he woke, he saw that branches had grown from Adaire's arms. The thick wood was reaching through the steel walls, forcing the metal to crumble and break. Dylan could smell damp earth and the overwhelming scent of fresh leaves.

He sat watching, his mouth open. Adaire's power was astonishing. He'd forgotten what it was like to be around other Fae.

All around the hole vines came through from the other side, roots growing into the metal, damaging it and enlarging the hole. One of the cold iron bars was already broken.

There was also banging going on, but the noise was masked, just as he had masked the sound of the water and Adaire was hiding the noise of breaking metal. Dylan could both hear it because he was Fae, and not hear it at the same time.

It must be a stone Fae.

He shivered at the effort it must cost them to ignore the pain the cruel cold iron was inflicting on all of them.

Egan was still working on the other wall, flaming it and trying to melt it down. Skye was making wind and fanning his flames.

Adaire withdrew her energy from the wall and came to sit down. Her body returned to normal, the tree branches disappeared. Through the hole in the wall flowed the two water spirits. Then the earth spirits came through, having to shift into vines in order to make it through the hole.

When they were all in the same cell, the newcomers collapsed on the floor along with Adaire, returning to what must be their original forms.

There was another female dryad. With greenish skin, long flowing hair and she looked young. Maybe only a couple thousand years. Three at tops.

The male Fae was a stone spirit. Gray and angular with short cropped hair.

The two water spirits were both women. One was very young, perhaps younger than the dryads. She had turquoise skin and long grasslike hair. The undine looked like she belonged in a lake, blissfully floating gently on a gentle current.

The other was ancient. She was one of the old ones. And powerful, more than everyone else in the cell put together. She was of the ocean. Sea green skin on a squishy looking body, which he knew was covering up massively strong muscles. Her hair looked like a sea creature, long tentacles of an anemone perhaps.

Skye came over, trying to help them, one by one. Sharing her energy to support them.

After a time Egan stopped as well. Drained of energy. He came to lie down and rest. They all fell into deep sleep.

Chapter 13 — Egan

Egan woke to the sound of rushing water and the smell of salt. The three water Fae were working on the wall he'd been burning. With three of them, they must have recovered more quickly. The earth spirits were all sleeping, as was Skye.

Water rushed out of the Faes' hands, ran down the wall to the floor, then was sucked up by their webbed feet and recycled. Not a drop was lost.

He felt weak and cold. But lying on the floor wasn't helping him warm up. He huddled close to the others on the floor for warmth and sat watching the water spirits.

One was young for a Fae, an undine, perhaps a thousand years old.

The other water Fae, the elders, her power felt boundless. Not many of them had stayed in the world. Most elders had retreated into Faerie, unwilling to change their lives. Especially to help humans. Why hadn't this one stayed safely in Faerie?

The two new earth spirits, a male and female, were probably around three thousand years old. About the same as Dylan, Skye, Adaire and Egan.

When he'd warmed himself, Egan went and looked through the hole into the empty cell. He could see the walls were weakened on three other sides. He sent his consciousness into that weakness, seeking life on the other side of the walls. There was nothing there.

Then he realized that the older water spirit had absorbed all of the spirits which had left their bodies. That was one of the reasons why she was so powerful. She'd even had the skill to absorb and transmute fire and air, where the younger Fae in the cell with her hadn't.

He shivered.

She would be a fearsome enemy.

The earth spirits recovered. Skye was still out, having shared so much of her energy.

Egan went back to sit with her, keeping her warm.

Adaire and the other two earth Fae went to the wall and the water spirits moved away and huddled together, helping each other refresh.

Egan watched Adaire do what she'd done before. She moved sections of the wall which were almost microscopic. Her work would be almost invisible, except that he could see daylight streaming through in the places she'd moved. The other two earth spirits watched and then joined in.

Eventually, the hole was large enough for a hand to fit through.

All of a sudden they stopped.

Egan heard the yelling of coarse voices.

The elder water spirit rushed over to the wall and Egan watched a sheen of glamour pass over it, making the hole disappear.

Skye woke and stood, wobbling from grogginess. She rushed over to help the elder, who looked very weak still.

An awful smell wafted through the hole. The smell of sweat, shit and a thousand unwashed bodies. Egan pinched his nose, willing himself not to breathe it in.

The voices still carried on.

"Hey, look what we caught," said one.

A cow bellowed loudly.

"Nice," said a deep, rough voice, which boomed through the cell. "Gut it before you put it over the fire."

"Naw, that'll spoil it."

"Balor is your King," said a woman, snarling.

"It's been so long since we've been together, I'd almost forgotten," said the first voice.

"Well, what will it take to make you remember?" said the deep voice.

"I'll gut the cow. I saw Elatha and Dela coming up the hill. They'll be here soon," said the first man.

The voices grew fainter as if moving off into the distance.

The elder slumped to the ground, shivering. Her face was filled with fear.

"What is it?" asked Egan.

"Fomorians. We've been captured by Fomorians. They were...dead."

The undine asked, "What is a Fomorian?"

"The old gods. Primeval spirits of the elements. They've got more raw power than you'll ever see in your life. They control the winds, the sea, the rain, movement of the earth, volcanos, plagues, famine, drought, everything. What we can do is nothing compared to them," said the elder.

"Then there's no hope?" said the dryad.

"We have to escape and soon," said the stone spirit.

"They'll roast the cow, feast and probably sleep. If we've broken through by then, perhaps we can pass by them," said the elder.

They took turns working on the wall and keeping their work hidden should any of the Fomorians pass by again.

Finally, they'd enlarged the hole enough so that they could pass through. All of them rested until the Fomorians went to sleep, except the stone spirit, Pearce. He used his glamour to cover the hole, making it look invisible from the outside.

Chapter 14 ❦ Skye

Skye woke from a dream of flying over mountain ranges. They were tall, the snow brightly lit the rising sun. Almost blinding. The dazzling snow was a peach color from the sunrise.

She came back to this world in the cell. Pearce stood over her, touching her arm to wake her quietly.

The cell was dark and smelly from too many bodies. The water spirits smelled the worst. They needed to be in water occasionally or they became stagnant. The elder had the most power and she really stank.

Skye stood, dazed. She walked over to the hole and began using her glamour to hide it while Pearce woke the others. The hole was big enough to slip their flexible bodies through, but it didn't do much for air circulation.

As an air spirit, she was especially sensitive to smells and lack of fresh air.

Skye wove a spell making the wall seamless. The hole disappeared, no sound from the inside reached out.

She heard no voices outside the cell, only an occasional snore. But the sleeper wasn't close. She could smell the incoming air. It was fresher than that of the cell, but still it was partly trapped, stale air. They must be inside a building of some sort.

She could smell the Formorians' unwashed bodies. Her nose told her they were inside a building, but there were air leaks. The sweet fragrance of lilacs drifted in from somewhere outside the building. And the sea. She could smell that too.

Skye took her mind through the hole and searched. There was nothing alive close by, other than several Fomorians. It was almost dawn. She could hear robins and blackbirds singing, frogs calling outside.

There were nine large iron cells. Her consciousness hovered above them now. On the other side, she saw seven huge bodies lying around sleeping. One was slumped against a building support post.

The Fomorians were giants. The old tales she'd heard as a child had always downplayed their size and intelligence. They were gods, but not as crafty as the Fae, who had overthrown them.

History was written by the winners.

And yet here they were, still alive and killing Fae. So they hadn't perished like all the old stories claimed.

Skye saw an opening in the building not far from the hole in their cell. She hovered around, looking for any other Fomorians still awake, but saw none. So sure of themselves, they'd left no guard.

She returned to her body in the cold iron cell.

Everyone was awake and up.

Skye whispered to them where to go.

The plan was for all of them to return to Faerie. To take the news back. Perhaps then a rescue party could be mounted to see if any Fae survived in the other cells.

They'd decided to travel in their own bodies. It would be faster than taking human form again. Even if, as it seemed, they could be tracked by the Fomorians more easily.

Skye was the first out. She became pure air leaking out through the hole, before returning to her own form.

She put her glamour over the others as they left the cell.

The two dryads became vines, their tendrils slithering through the opening and hitting the concrete floor in front of the cell. Then the back part of the vines followed through the hole and Adaire and Glenna reformed into their Fae bodies, greenish, tall and strong.

The water spirits poured through the opening, flowing out, one at a time. Then each pool reformed as Dylan, Meredith and Lynette in their squishy looking, strong bodies.

Egan became a salamander who climbed up the wall, through the hole and down, before returning to himself.

Pearce, the stone Fae became lean and thin, then turned into molten lava, pouring out the whole before solidifying into himself again.

They ran across the aisle between the cells and the wall of the building, hugged the wall down to the opening and slid out. She too slipped out.

They all moved towards the cover of some nearby tall glossy bushes.

"The sea is that direction," said Meredith, the elder, pointing her webbed finger. "It's not far."

"Faerie lies that way," said Glenna, the female earth spirit from the other cell. She pointed in the opposite direction.

Egan asked, "Should we split up or stay together?"

Pearce said, "We need to find out where we are. How close are we to Faerie?"

Skye said, "We need to keep moving. We don't know when they'll wake. And they're giants. They'll cover a lot of ground."

"I think we should split up," said Dylan. "We water spirits will slow all of you down. We need to cleanse ourselves. We can probably swim faster to Faerie than we could walk. Even if it's the long way around."

Meredith nodded.

Lynette, the young water spirit shrugged her shoulders.

Adaire said, "I don't know."

Glenna said, "It makes no difference to me as long as we go now."

Egan said, "Okay, water spirits go. We'll meet you in Faerie. Whoever gets there first, sends help for the other group. And to see if there's any living Fae we've left behind."

Dylan nodded.

Skye watched as Dylan, Meredith and Lynette moved off in the direction of the sea. Their webbed feet must have made it difficult to run. Their gaits were uneven as they travelled through the long grass.

Egan, Glenna, Adaire and Pearce scrambled through the brush up a rise, trying to get as far as they could quickly, from the old building that had contained their prison.

Skye said, "I'm flying until dawn. That will help me get my strength back and help us decide which way to go."

She slid into the air, curving upwards. Above the tops of trees, scattering the dawn singing birds. The light was just barely skimming the horizon.

Down below she could see abandoned factories and farms. She couldn't tell where they were. There was a smallish town and rural countryside. But no large cities anywhere nearby. She swooped down and sat, invisible, in a tree near a street for a few minutes and looked at license plates between the blinding headlights. She saw New York, Vermont, New Hampshire and Maine. There could have been others, but a big dog wandering by began to bark at her. Skye sped away.

She reveled in the feel of the cool air sliding past her body. How long had she been held prisoner?

Drawing strength from the use of her body, she flew over the treetops and back out into the countryside over where her friends were passing through a pasture that stank of fresh cow manure. The reddish brown and white cows stood and stared at the Fae, looking slightly confused as they chewed the new green grass.

There was still no sign of the giants when dawn came and she set down just ahead of the other Fae.

They were walking through an area with a few tall trees and a lot of shrubs and tall grasses. It was wildish, as far away from people as they could get. Two deer grazing the underbrush stood and stared at them. Some sweet smelling shrub was blooming. Skye didn't know any of the plants in this part of the world.

"Where are we?" asked Egan, as they continued walking.

"I'm not sure. Somewhere in the Northeast. I saw license plates for New York, Vermont, New Hampshire and Maine. The Atlantic's off in the distance. It must cut closer in farther south, where the water spirits went."

"So, how do we cross the water?" asked Glenna.

"I've lived as a human for six years," said Egan. "The Fomorians didn't catch me. Dylan had the same experience. We were caught when we weren't wearing human bodies. I think that masks our identity enough that they can't find or catch us."

Adaire said, "Same with me. I was caught when I was in my real form. I think Egan's right. We need to become humans again."

"That'll sap our strength. We can travel faster if we're Fae," said Pearce.

"Yes, but we'll be safer," said Skye.

"So, how do we cross?" asked Glenna, again.

"Boat?" asked Adaire.

"Plane," said Skye.

Egan said, "We need to buy passports and ID from someone. We'll need money."

"Passports and ID for five people," said Pearce.

"I can steal money," said Skye.

"Enough to buy us ID's, passports and airfare?" asked Pearce.

"I don't know it I can stand being up in a plane," said Glenna.

"It'll be shorter than a boat ride," said Adaire. "We need to get to Faerie as soon as possible. They've got to be told what's happening."

"We'll be right beside you," said Pearce.

Glenna nodded, her green face pale in the rising sun.

Egan said, "We should take cover soon. We don't want to be seen by humans or to have to use glamour to disguise ourselves. I think all of us are too weak."

Skye felt invigorated by flying, better than she had since being captured. But she needed to rest, needed food. She was still weak.

"Where?" asked Pearce. "The trees haven't leafed out yet. It's far too bare here.

They kept walking for a couple hours before they came to an abandoned house with peeling white paint. It sat surrounded by tall evergreen hedges. The barn and several outbuildings had long since fallen down into piles of rotting lumber.

It was on the outskirts of a small town. Several homes in the area were abandoned, many with for sale signs. This one looked more private because of the hedge.

The house was maybe ten years old, the windows boarded up with warped plywood. They broke in through a back door. It looked like they were the first ones to do so. The house was empty of furniture. There was no water or electricity. The builders hadn't even finished the kitchen or bath.

They sat on the off white living room carpet in the bare white room.

Skye hated the chemical smell of the carpet, but it was the best they could do.

After they'd rested, they each began the long, slow process of creating a human shell to live inside of.

Skye sat by the boarded up window. Someone hadn't done a great job measuring the wood. It didn't cover the window completely so fresh air flowed in through the broken glass.

She took strength from the air and used it in her work, creating cells, a skeleton, tendons, muscles, capillaries, veins, nerves and all the other things that allowed her to make a functioning human body to live within.

Folding in her wings, she formed the human body around her own, making it so that she could slip out when necessary.

Several hundred years ago, when she'd first learned this type of magic, no one, not even in Faerie had known about cells and the inner workings of human bodies. But Skye found the more she learned, the better the body would function for her. That was one of the things that had led her to study the human body and massage therapy to begin with.

The body she chose to create was strong and muscular. Fast and lean. She would need those things if the Fomorians caught up with them.

She was counting on that not happening.

But Meredith had been terrified of the giants. Said she'd been alive during that long, long war. She knew what they were capable of.

But she didn't have time to tell the others the long story, not before they split up. She said getting back to Faerie was more important.

Were they really as fearsome as she thought? After all, the Fae had conquered them.

Or had they?

Chapter 15 ❦ Meredith

Meredith wove through the brambles, the sharp thorns tearing her skin. She kept running, even though her breath came in gasps now.

The salt, fish and kelpy scents of the sea drew her forward. Filled her with more strength than she thought possible. Dylan and Lynette were ahead of her. Not too far, but they were younger.

She squinted in the bright sunlight. How long had they been trapped in that cold iron cell? Her eyes weren't used to light anymore. Brightness had always been a challenge for her, she was born to be in the dimly lit ocean, not moving quickly across the land.

They ran for miles and miles. Through dry brush and drier pastures. Avoiding the small towns they passed along the way. She didn't want them to be seen. They probably should have taken the time to create human bodies to hide in. But Meredith wasn't sure they had the time to spare.

And they would be able to run swifter in their natural forms.

Even on land the water spirits were much faster than humans. Faster than cheetahs even. But not faster than the dryads, fire spirits or the sylphs.

And certainly not faster than the Fomorians.

The giants were the winds, the rain, the very elements of the earth. The old gods were strong. Meredith had never really believed the old tales that said they were dead.

You couldn't kill the wind. Or the ocean.

She tested the others.

"*Can you hear me?*" she spoke silently, to their minds.

"*Yes,*" said Dylan, to her mind. He fell back beside her, Lynette followed.

"Yes," said Lynette out loud. Her name meant little lake. She was young, but she would always be a little lake, not a powerful ocean. "I can hear, but I can't send."

"Good, at least there are two of us who can send," said Meredith.

They kept running, the sharp stones slicing the soft webbing of their feet. Meredith kept the pace up. She knew what the giants were capable of. Once at sea, there would be fewer of them. She hoped they hadn't woken *Her*.

Perhaps if they went far north, stayed close to land, they could avoid *Her*.

By midday they crouched on a high bluff overlooking the ocean. Meredith reveled in the fishy smell. The bay was filled with fishing boats.

She unsheathed and flexed her razor sharp claws.

She pointed to the rocky cliffs. There were wide crevices, they could climb down unnoticed and slip into the sea.

"*Stay close to me,* " she said, silently. "*There will be nets in the water.*"

The climb down was long and tricky. She felt the wind blow past the rocks.

Searching.

Panic streaked through her body.

One of the Fomorians. She didn't know which one. It had been so long since she'd seen them. And she'd hoped to never see them again.

The others felt it too, flattening into cracks in the stone wall.

Became sea spray on the rocks of the cliff.

No one breathed.

The wind slipped past, not noticing them.

It took hours to climb down to the sea. Meredith's hands and feet were cut and bleeding from the sharp rocks. She ignored the pain and searched for the next foothold.

The sea was so close. But they couldn't jump. Too many sharp rocks. And the water here was too shallow.

An early fog crept in just as they touched the water.

Cethlenn.

Meredith wouldn't mention her name out loud or even send it to the others. That would draw Cethlenn's attention.

She slid through the water quickly, followed by the others. The fog couldn't penetrate the surface of the water.

They streaked through the large bay filled with nets. Meredith sliced those that she could, freeing the fish trapped within. She didn't know the names of the fish, this wasn't her home. The plants and fish were strange to her.

The fish followed them, racing away from the nets, hopefully to safety.

Would the fish serve as camouflage?

She wasn't sure.

The sea gave all of them strength, infusing them with her water and they used it to gain speed and strength. Racing along the sea floor, trying to avoid any ships above. The farther from shore they got, the deeper the water, the dimmer the light. But the current kept the water relatively unpolluted.

They swam without resting. For hours upon hours. It took two days before they reached a series of islands which must be part of Canada.

Meredith wished they'd been able to take the Gulf Stream and cross the ocean there. But in that ridge lay an abyss. Where *She* dwelled. Domnu. The mother of the Fomorians.

They couldn't risk waking *Her*.

Better to take the long way around.

So they swam through areas where there was lots of human traffic. Too many boats that filled the sea with their noise. With their engine oil. With their filth, feces and garbage. Close to land.

There were also more predators.

The seals were massive and fierce.

They could outrun one or two, but in the dimly lit waters, the creatures seemed to come out of nowhere.

Water Fae had good vision in the darkness, but still the seals were so much faster.

One male had been ten feet long and must have weighed around four hundred pounds. He was extraordinarily fast and caught them unawares.

He came out from behind an old sunken boat. He was on them in seconds. The seal caught one of Lynette's fins in his mouth. Meredith spun around. Attacking him. Slashing his face with her claws.

The bull let go. Dylan dragged Lynette away. Meredith followed.

So did the bull.

Meredith raked him with her claws again. Screeching underwater.

He was stopped. Either from the pain or unnerved by the noise.

Either way, he swam off to find easier prey.

They left the area quickly. After much searching, Meredith found a long strip of the sea weed she was looking for. She tore it loose and bound Lynette's torn lateral fin to her body. She'd swim crookedly, but at least it would have a chance to heal. The fin was still bleeding. Causing too much attention from the surrounding sea life. They didn't need to attract sharks.

The three of them moved on, exhausted, they couldn't stay in one place long. How many days had it been since they left the cells? Three, four, a week. Meredith had lost all sense of time. The sea did that to one. Time meant nothing here.

Not like in the human world.

As they swam farther north, the water grew noticeably colder. Water spirits could handle the cold. But soon there might be ice above them. She didn't know how far south the ice had come this winter. How fast it might be receding.

It seemed like spring. The water grew cloudy as they moved north. It was cloudy with phytoplankton and plankton. Whales gathered to dine.

It had been days since they'd escaped from the Fomorians. They were at least that many days away from Faerie.

Beneath the surface it was difficult for Meredith to figure out where they were in relation to what she knew of the land. She could feel exactly where Faerie was and could've swam a direct line there. But hugging the coastlines was a different thing.

They rose to the surface, trying to get their bearings. Fog surrounded the coast.

Cethlenn's scent was on the breeze. The taste of Corb was in the seawater, but Meredith felt he hadn't sensed them.

They dove for deeper water and stayed away from the land, but out of the deeps as well.

They'd reached the southern tip of Greenland.

Had the Formians known she'd choose this route? Or were they simply searching everywhere? That was unlike them. Perhaps they'd learned strategy after all this time.

The three of them found a sunken ship where nothing seemed to be living, besides shellfish. It was fairly modern, maybe ten or fifteen years old and smallish. The cabin barely large enough for the three of them.

They rested.

Meredith unbound Lynette's fin. At least the bleeding had stopped, but the fin hung useless and limp. Neither she nor Dylan were healers.

Lynette would just have to keep up.

After this short rest, they'd need to sprint again.

Chapter 16 ✦ Egan

Egan stood at the crowded bar. His human body made him feel sluggish. Thumping dance music blared over the sound system so loudly, he could barely hear people around him speak.

He basked in the warmth of the room, wearing a silky black shirt, black jeans and black shoes. She'd bought them at a discount store with money she'd stolen. They didn't have to last for long.

Just long enough to get to Faerie.

He inhaled the alcohol, perfume and aftershave tinged air. Humans hunting for sex or connection.

Skye made her way round the dance floor, swirling with the music, wearing a filmy black dress with a long blue scarf that whirled with her. She'd created a human body that was beautiful and svelte. Long blonde hair and just enough curves to keep human men watching her breasts and not her hands.

She reached her long slender fingers into pockets, filching wallets without anyone knowing. And sliding them into a flat fabric purse she wore over one shoulder and across her body. Such was the gift of a sylph.

This was the second club they'd gone through tonight. Egan slowly sipped his tequila, waiting. Not making eye contact with anyone.

The short, squat man he'd spoken to earlier said he'd known someone. Another man who could get him what they needed. The short man, Antonio was his name, had gone outside to use his cell. It was too noisy in here.

Egan fingered the burner phone he'd bought with Skye's stolen money in his pocket. It felt strange to have a phone again. He'd had one in Santa Fe. Couldn't run a business without one.

Egan watched the dancers. Mostly couples, but there were a few women dancing by themselves. And a couple of men trying to catch the attention of women. Unsuccessfully.

He ignored the blond who was trying to catch his. He had no interest in a casual sexual liaison with a human.

Antonio came back up to the bar. He smelled of cigarette smoke.

"Samuel's on his way over to talk to you. He's just down the street at Sashay."

"Great. Thank you."

"You're a real gentleman, ya' know that? Where you from?"

"Santa Fe."

"The Southwest. I want to go there. Warm weather all the time. Desert. Sounds nice."

Egan laughed, "Twenty degrees in the winter, ninety in the summer."

"Really, so it's just like here." Antonio's face drooped in disappointment

"Not as much moisture though."

"Damn. It thought it stayed warmer in the winter."

"You're thinking of L.A, probably."

"Yeah. Oh look, there's Samuel."

Antonio pointed to a tall pale man, dressed all in scarlet, who entered the bar. With an entourage. Two huge bulky guys, one black and one Latino. Either one of whom could benchpress Egan with one hand.

Antonio walked up to them and said, "Let's get a table."

Egan said, "Sure."

Egan took his tequila along and sat on one edge of the semi-circular booth across from Samuel. Antonio had disappeared. The black bodyguard stood nearby, the Latino sat on the other edge of the booth. Samuel sat at the center, eyes on the door. Clearly he wanted to see everything and keep his back to the wall.

But it wasn't the safest place for Samuel to be. He certainly couldn't get out of the booth quickly and run. Egan guessed the man didn't feel that threatened, he was too cocky. Stupid.

"Antonio tells me you need some documentation," said Samuel, tapping a cigarette on the table before lighting it.

"Yes, I and my business associates are in need of ID's and passports."

"How many?"

"There are five of us."

"You'll need photos."

"Yes, we have them," said Egan.

"You realize this is an expensive endeavor. We're talking seven grand each person for ID and passport. Cash in advance."

Egan said, "I can get the money to you in a couple of days."

"When do you need them?"

"As soon as possible. We have business in the UK."

"International huh? What business you in, if you don't mind me asking?"

"We're in the surveillance business."

"Good money in that?"

"Not as much as I'd like," said Egan.

"Well, if you're ever back this way, text me. I'm always looking for fresh blood."

"I'll do that," said Egan, keeping his emotions off his face.

No way would he get within ten feet of this pompous ass.

Samuel gave him the number to text when Egan had the cash. Egan filed the number on his phone under contacts.

Then he shook hands with Samuel and got up, leaving the table. He sent a thought to Skye silently.

"Done here. Let's move on."

"On my way," she sent back.

He went outside into the cool, fresh air and stood on the sidewalk.

Skye joined him shortly.

They walked along the sidewalk.

"How'd we do tonight?" he asked.

"Better than last night. People in this area carry more cash than in the other town. And they drink heavier. Easier to fleece. We can count it when we get back."

"We need $35,000 for passports and ID."

"Another night should get us there."

"Then we'll have to buy plane tickets."

"We'll need a prepaid credit card. Don't want to use cash. Too many questions," she said.

He nodded and they continued walking along the sidewalk of the small touristy town, dimly lit by streetlights.

Two men were following them. Egan decided they were probably armed.

He let Skye know.

Humans couldn't do a lot of harm to Fae bodies, but he and Skye were in human bodies. They could still move faster than most humans and hit harder. A bullet would be a major setback though.

They decided to hide instead of fight. Before they got to the next corner, they slipped down a narrow passageway between two buildings. One was an old house refitted into a shop. Once behind it, they began to climb.

The house was made of wood. Egan stood still for a moment. He drew some power up from the earth. Felt the magic flow through him and then made his human fingers form suction cups, allowing him to stick slightly to the wood.

He scrambled up the back of the house before the goons made it to the alley. Skye was faster than he was. They crouched next to a dormer on the roof, hidden in the shadows and by their glamour.

The two men looked up and down the alley, then split up, one walking each direction, guns pulled and expecting to find someone hiding there. Finally, they came back together and stood talking.

"Tell me again why we're after these two."

"Boss said they had lots of cash. Wanted us to follow them. Find out where they're staying. Get the cash."

"Where could they have gone?"

"Dunno. Into one of the shops?"

The other man said nothing.

"Damn. Samuel's gonna kill us."

"Nothin' to do about it. Let's get back to the bar."

The two men walked down the alley a bit and disappeared between two buildings.

Skye moved and Egan put his arm in front of her.

"Not yet," he sent. *"They gave up too easily, don't you think?"*

Fog drifted down from the bluff just above the town.

Egan shivered and dropped the glamour completely, becoming as human as possible.

He watched Skye do the same.

Cethlenn was here.

105

Chapter 17 — Balor

Balor stood in the leafless forest overlooking the town. It wasn't much camouflage. Giants weren't easy to disguise. He wasn't like Cethlenn who could change into fog or Conand who became the wind. He was blazing hot drought. Out of place in this landscape.

He hated the calls of the woodland birds and the spring buds on trees. He belonged to the heat of summer, when there was no water. He longed to wither plants and watch animals die of thirst.

Of course he could make that landscape here, but he wasn't staying long enough. Just passing through. No, he'd save that for Faerie.

When the Fae had escaped he'd checked the other traps. None left alive. He'd lost all his hostages, as well as his playthings.

But perhaps this was better.

He stomped on a butterfly fluttering around the white bloodroot flowers at his feet. Annoying things, butterflies. Reminded him of Fae.

But the escaped Fae might lead him to Faerie. He was sure that's where they were headed. To warn Faerie about his people. He was equally sure they thought he and his kind were all dead.

They'd soon learn the truth.

The old gods would never die.

They couldn't be killed.

He smiled and waited for Cethlenn or the others to return with news.

Corb had caught the scent of the water Fae and followed them out to sea. They hadn't bothered to make human bodies, like the others. They'd be easy to follow.

There were a few other old ones he needed to collect. Still slumbering. Once they were awake, once they found Faerie, then the fun would really begin.

They would see destruction the like of which Faerie never experienced before.

Chapter 18 ☙ Fiachna

The rain drenched his heavy wool cloak. The air was scented with freshness. The sky so dark it looked like dusk even at midday. The land still holding the cold barrenness of winter.

Fiachna stared at the ruined grave. It looked the same as the last two. Boulders strewn everywhere. The turf torn off of them. Bare earth showing. Scattered bones exposed to the elements.

One side of this barrow threatening to cave in.

The smell of unwashed bodies and feces lingered. He couldn't place the smell though. Not human, not any animal he recognized. It stank though, all the same.

Fiachna went inside and put everything in its place.

"My Luminary, I am so sorry your grave has been disturbed like this."

He reset the large stones with his magic. Placing them just so, restoring the balance of the structure, making it whole again.

Then he tied the boundary of Faerie back into the stones. He felt the energy move through the boundary with a pinging sound. It was functional again.

He stepped outside the barrow.

Again he felt the presence of something ominous. A presence he hadn't felt since he was young. Fiachna shivered with dread and felt a heaviness that couldn't be lightened by the oncoming spring.

But it couldn't be. They were all dead.

He called a raven, feeling its talons pinch the skin on his forearm.

He told it the message to deliver.

It flew off into the darkness of the day.

He sealed off the tomb and checked the boundary again. It held.

It was past time others began walking the edges. He couldn't do this alone.

Something was terribly wrong.

Chapter 19 ✦ Dylan

Dylan swam through the gray green sea water. How many days since they'd escaped? He'd lost all sense of time. That was the way of the ocean.

His muscles ached and he didn't remember ever being so weary. All he could do was swing his arms forward again and again, his legs always kicking. Trying to stay alert and extend his senses as far as they would reach. Searching for danger in whatever form it might take.

Seals, sharks, Fomorians.

They swam relentlessly through the dimly lit water, staying as deep as they dared. Not stopping to rest for long. Eating when they could.

Knowing there was no safety until they reached Faerie.

They'd passed out of Canadian waters and turned east to Greenland. The water felt much colder here. It tasted less salty, perhaps the snowmelt was diluting the salt.

Beneath the waves it was murky. The water was filled with life, microscopic and larger.

They were still trying to avoid seals. And fishing boats. The swim was grueling.

After years of living mostly out of water, Dylan found he missed smelling paint. And the variety of sound. He loved being underwater, but they had no time to stop and enjoy just being. No time to explore.

Meredith led, she was the one who knew the ocean this far north.

Dylan swam, following Meredith and helping keep Lynette on course. She swam crookedly with her damaged fin and had to work much harder than they did just to swim in a straight line.

So he swam close to her, helping her along with a gentle push every few strokes.

They stopped every so often and rested They had all grown tired of constant swimming.

The only thing that made it worthwhile was that so far, they'd escaped attention from the Fomorians.

Occasionally, Meredith sent messages to Lynette and him. Telling them stories of when she was young and about the war between the Fomorians and the Fae's ancestors.

The war which was obviously still happening.

When he'd been born, the war was a distant memory and no one ever spoke of the Fomorians.

How could Faerie have thought such a foe was conquered?

Arrogant fools.

Would any of them take the threat seriously before it was too late?

"Are we stopping on Greenland?" he sent to Meredith.

"No time. We must move on before the Fomorians catch up with us again. They'll find we haven't gone directly across and come up north. And they move faster than we can even imagine."

He sighed.

If he survived, if Faerie survived, if humans survived. If he was very fortunate, someday, he'd be able to paint again.

Chapter 20 ⋄ Skye

Skye perched on the roof of the house. Egan crouched on the other side of the window which jutted out and at least gave them a little cover. As soon as they sensed the Fomorian, they had shut down their glamour or else their magic would help Cethlenn find them.

Without it, she hoped, they just seemed like two humans.

Perched on the roof of a house and hiding.

She hoped the two thugs were gone. If the two had bothered to look up, Skye was sure she and Egan were totally visible.

But the fog was swirling through the town, maybe the Fomorian would hide them a little, disconcerting as if felt.

She looked around. It might be possible to slide down a drainpipe. If it held. But probably not without making noise. And if the two goons were still around…

They couldn't make their fingers sticky, couldn't use any magic. Not with the Fomorian around.

Nothing to do, but wait until the Fomorian was gone. Then use their glamour to sneak out of town and back to the others.

And find another town.

Another place to get ID's. And more money for the plane tickets.

She sat down on the roof. And still, hanging on to the dormer with one hand, closed her eyes. She began to clear her head, let things drift away.

"What are you doing?" whispered Egan.

"Meditating."

"This is no time to meditate."

"It's the best time to meditate. It'll clear my head. Help me think better. You should try it."

"You're crazy."

He said nothing more, but she could feel him over there, restless and anxious.

She focused on her breathing.

When she opened her eyes again, the fog had lifted. The Fomorian was gone.

"Let's go," she said. They needed to get away from humans. Humans with guns. Who could cause no end of trouble for them.

"How?"

"Use our power and slide down that drainpipe. And race out of town."

"The Fomorian? The goons?"

"I think they're gone. The goons won't see us if we use our glamour."

"I'm more worried about the Fomorians," he said.

"Me too. But I'm not sure the thugs have gone. I don't want to attract their attention either."

"Okay, we'll do it your way. But only use our magic until we're a few blocks away. The fog might not be the only one around."

"Okay."

She gathered up all her power and scurried across the roof to the corner farthest away from the gap between the two buildings that they'd come through.

Beneath the roof, curving back towards the building ran a drainpipe. It was older. Stronger metal than the newer aluminum style ones. It might hold them.

Skye allowed herself to drift down, trying to take her weight off the pipe with her magic. Not quite flying, but becoming lighter than normal. Being her true self, nearly weightless and able to fly. Not like this heavy, human body.

She touched down on the ground and stood back, signaling to Egan.

He slid down quickly, the pipe wrenching free at the last moment with a metallic screech.

They pulled out their glamour, making themselves blend into the background surrounding them and ran down the alley. The opposite direction they'd last seen the thugs.

"What was that?" a deep voice said.

She smelled cigarette smoke.

"What?" said another male voice.

"I heard metal. And footsteps."

Damn, they hadn't muffled their feet.

They did now.

The thugs ran towards them for awhile, but soon stopped. She knew the men couldn't see them in the darkness. Or hear them.

Six blocks later, they dropped the glamour, but kept running.

Skye was glad she'd worn flats to the bar. Heels would never have worked.

It took them twenty minutes to run the ten miles back to the house. Through woods and heavy brush. Faster than humans, inside their human looking bodies. It felt like a very long time to remain invisible. They let the glamour drop a mile before the house.

When they arrived, Adaire met them at the door.

"What happened? Why didn't you come home last night?"

"Fomorians. And thugs," said Egan.

"We've got to get out of here," said Skye. She picked the money out of the wallets and left them behind. The money she rolled up, wrapped in a cloth and returned to her fabric bag

They quickly threw the few clothes and belongings they'd collected into daypacks and left the abandoned house.

Chapter 21 ⚬ Meredith

Meredith and the others stopped briefly on Iceland. Resting on a deserted rocky beach filled with huge boulders. There was a road up above and they could hear the occasional car or motorcycle go by. The sky looked slate gray. Clouds filled with rain. She could smell the storm coming in, taste the unsalted water. Everything felt damp and welcoming.

Meredith wanted to just lie on damp, soft grass, looking up at the sun. Let her aching, weary muscles rest. She'd spent too long hiding in a human body. She was unused to being in the sea for this long.

That saddened her. Then again, she wasn't just being. She was fleeing and hiding.

They hadn't seen any sign of the Fomorians since leaving Canada. That worried her.

Either they'd assumed the Fae would take the shortest route and had gone straight over the Atlantic. Or worse.

They were following them and Meredith simply couldn't sense them.

It was possible the Fomorians had gone on ahead. And that they stood blocking any entrance to Faerie.

Lynette was examining her torn fin. Nothing was going to fix it now. If they'd been in Faerie they might have found a healer. Not out here in the wilds though.

Meredith sighed and watched the undine. Lynette was so young, so innocent. It had been a very long time since Meredith had met so trusting a soul.

An arctic breeze passed over them, chilling her wet body.

Dylan looked restless. He climbed on the boulders, going nowhere. He was young too. Didn't know how to rest.

"We should move on," said Meredith.

"I thought you wanted us to rest," Dylan said.

"Are you resting?" she asked.

"Sorry," he said, coming to sit with them.

"Sometime before we reach Faerie, I expect we'll meet the Fomorians."

"I thought they were in North America," said Lynette, her lovely face crumpling.

"No dear, they are everywhere. And if they find us, they'll try to stop us from entering Faerie."

Meredith paused, looking at their faces, waiting for it to sink in.

"Will they be in the water?" asked Lynette.

"Most likely, and on land and air as well. We must either sneak past them or fight. Are you willing to try?"

"Yes," said Dylan, without hesitation.

"I'll try," said Lynette. "My magic isn't the strongest, though."

"It will get stronger, closer to Faerie. And you were strong enough to make a human body."

"Not a good one though. I think my energy leaked through. That's how they found me in San Francisco," she said, staring at her torn fin.

"Can you change yourself into a pike, or salmon or trout?" asked Meredith.

"Yes, I can," said Lynette.

"Good, then if we sense the Fomorians, please do so immediately. And swim like hell to Faerie. Do not stop to rest or for food. Just swim and tell them everything."

"Where will you be?" asked Lynette.

"Dylan and I will be right behind you, if we can. We may have to stay and divert them. We'll just have to wait and see what happens."

She nodded.

"What about you?" she asked Dylan.

"I can fight, some. But how do you fight fog?"

"You go beneath the water, where fog cannot live."

"How do you fight the sea?"

"That's more difficult. You can use glamour. Make them think you're not Fae. The best thing to do is to not let them find you in the first place. The Fomorians are more powerful than any of us. Our ancestors defeated them not by force but by trickery. Always trickery. They made friends with them, seduced them with our sweet mead, our cows' luscious cream, the delicate, rich pastries we could bake, the tender beef. We married the smaller, less powerful ones and their children became ours, we stole some of their magic that way. That strengthened us. Eventually, the more powerful ones, the old gods, wearied of life and faded away. Perhaps the weaker ones were killed. Or so most in Faerie thought."

Dylan nodded.

"Come, this is the last long part of our journey. We swim."

It took two long days and nights for them to reach the northwest coast of Ireland. Another day to follow to the coast southward, until they found the right outlet.

When they caught the taste of fresh water, that's when Meredith sensed Corb and Domnu.

Right behind them.

Chasing them up the Shannon.

Chapter 22 ·☙· Adaire

Adaire trudged along behind the others. Glenna and Pearce walked directly ahead of her. Their arms interwoven, heads together. They'd chosen to walk on a bike path beside the road cutting through the forest.

The sun streaming through the new spring growth of the maple trees filled her heart. It could only have been better if she wasn't lugging around this human body on the outside of her own. But she was.

She loved the smell of the leaves, sweet and green. The flashes of brown, reds and yellows as birds flitted between branches. The deep throated jungle call of the pileated woodpecker mingled with the chicka-dee-dee-dee of the small gray, black and white birds. A hummingbird buzzed past her head.

Adaire felt tired. Dryads normally stayed in one forest, they didn't wander far. She just wanted to stay in one place and be.

She didn't want to travel from town to town, then be shut up in some stuffy abandoned building while Egan and Skye tried to get the necessary money and IDs. She certainly wasn't looking forward to getting on a plane.

A boat wasn't ideal either. That's how she'd gotten to the U.S. in the first place, hundreds of years ago. It had been awful.

Perhaps she should have stayed in Faerie.

She tried to remember why she'd left. But it was so long ago. She'd lived so many human lives since then. Learning new skills, learning how to be with humans, how to talk to them. Even how their systems worked.

Faerie had seemed rotten somehow. Like an apple filled with bruising at the core, but no visible signs as to why that should be so. And then there was the loss of Ashleigh. She hadn't been able to bear that. Not and stay in Faerie. Adaire had exiled herself out into the world to be miserable and grieve.

What would they find when they returned?

Would anything have changed?

A car raced by them, loud music blaring through the closed windows. The smelly exhaust lingered long after the car had gone by.

Skye and Egan were in front. Arguing, as they often did. This time it was about which way to go.

"I think we should head East. Towards the coast," said Skye.

"We already did that. We hit the two-bit tourist towns. They don't have the criminals we need. Yeah, you've gotten us a lot of money. But we need IDs. We need to go to a city," said Egan.

"There's no place to hide in a city," said Skye.

"We hide on the street. Just like the homeless."

"That's not safe," she said.

"With all of us together, we'll be fine. Safer than wandering out here, waiting for the Fomorians to find us."

"We haven't seen them for days."

"They aren't done with us yet," said Egan.

Adaire ignored their argument. Skye wouldn't hold out for long. She was a sylph. Fire always beat air. Always. Only water could slow down fire. Skye arguing with Egan just added wind to fan the flame.

Plus, he was right. They had enough money. To continue on with their plan, they needed IDs. Soon.

There was no guarantee that the water Fae would make it back to Faerie. No guarantee that any of them would. But they had to keep trying.

To do nothing, to fail, was unconscionable.

Chapter 23 ⚭ Dylan

Dylan swam against the current, following Meredith and Lynette up the river. Lynette had been strengthened by the fresh water. If one could call it that. Her magic had never been really strong.

He tasted solvents and manure, fuel and other chemicals. The surface water was alive with boat traffic. Huge cargo ships and even a couple of cruise ships.

Dolphins played around their bows.

They kept well away from the dolphins.

There were few fish here, where once there had been thousands. He used to live here. Now it was walled with concrete, turned into a port.

Nature had left this place.

He felt the pressure of Corb and Domnu behind them. The sea, pushing up the Shannon as the water flowed backwards.

And Domnu pulled at them. Trying to drag them back out to sea with every wave. How could anyone resist the strength of the Mother of the Fomorians?

But they had to.

They had to make it to Faerie.

Lynette turned into a very large salmon and slid upstream, hopefully unnoticed by the Fomorians. She passed Meredith. Her silvery scales flashed in the dim light as she disappeared around the bend.

"May you be the fastest fish in the river," he sent to her, hoping she was too far away to hear. Hopefully, she'd escape the dolphins.

"Shift," sent Meredith to him.

He did as he was told, turning into a salmon. He could swim faster this way, even though he felt clumsy and awkward. This body was better suited for speed. But it was ripe for predators.

They swam as quickly as they could, struggling against the warring currents. They switched back to their own bodies when another pod of dolphins appeared.

Breathing heavily and tired, Dylan swam on. The dolphins were still coming at them, as if not believing they weren't salmon.

One dolphin got too close and Dylan shot a blast of power at it, smacking the dolphin on the head. Meredith, also a salmon, opened her jaws, suddenly enormous, large enough to take in the entire dolphin's head. It veered away.

They kept swimming and after a time, Dylan decided his magic had become boring. Tame. Unsurprising and uninventive. Meredith had such an amazing imagination. He could learn a lot from her.

It seemed to take forever to get through the estuary and past all the ships. He could still feel Corb and Domnu behind them.

The Fomorians wouldn't have let them go without a huge battle, would they?

Or was this all part of a plan?

They'd just passed out of the estuary and through the city. Was it Limerick? Dylan thought so. It had been so long since he'd been here. The channel narrowed, filled with water grass, other fish and stringy little eels.

He snatched one up and ate it, relishing the fishy flavor. The water here tasted and smelled cleaner.

There was no sign of Lynette. She was lake born though and the youngest. She would still know the way back.

Hours later, they were still swimming when the sun set. The water grew so shallow in spots, it was easier to walk.

The evening air cooled their skins even farther. They saw an occasional human out walking, but the night was quiet.

Until the ground shook.

Meredith looked at him and said, "Earthquake. Tsunami."

He looked around. Panicked.

They ran for the highest hill they could reach.

Which wasn't very high.

A few seconds later another quake.

Then the sea water roared in around them.

Domnu had come to land. They kept on running, following the hill inland.

Dylan yelled, "Human!"

"What?"

"Switch to human! Now!"

"I can't, not that fast."

"Do it!" he yelled.

As he ran, he hastily constructed a human body. Male, long and lean. A runner. Athletic. It wouldn't be perfect, wouldn't last long, but he hoped it would be enough.

His breathing became ragged.

Meredith followed him, working on the change.

Finally, they both had to stop. But they kept

concentrating on creating the human bodies. They were exposed. Domnu lay beneath, waves raging at the foot of the hill.

He felt sure the other Fomorians were nearby. He couldn't smell them, rather Dylan sensed them, perceived their fury. If his senses weren't so masked by the inadequate body he was making, he could probably hear them.

When they'd caught their breath, and finished their human bodies, Dylan and Meredith ran again. Naked. Far into the night. Passing through fields of cows and cow manure. Their bare feet padding along asphalt roads and dirt paths. Farther and farther into the wilds.

Searching for the entrance to Faerie.

Chapter 24 ⋅⊚⋅ Egan

Egan stood in the boarding section of Aer Lingus in Boston, chewing cinnamon gum. Skye paced around the waiting area. Adaire, Glenna and Pearce stood in a corner, leaving the uncomfortable plastic seats to other passengers. The flight would be packed. The waiting area felt cold and drafty. He knew the plane would be no better. He wore a warm sweater underneath the leather jacket and corduroy pants. Very uncool looking, but warm.

A woman standing next to him was wearing too much perfume. It was very floral, but he also smelled sandalwood. Egan tried to suppress a sneeze and moved away from her.

He smiled. It had taken a week of searching, but they finally had five packets of ID's in hand. Fake passports, driver's licenses and credit cards. They'd also bought ferry tickets to England so as not to be denied entrance to Ireland by customs. Humans and their silly rules. They seemed to think the world could actually be separated by borders.

But he supposed the same could be said of Faerie, who'd closed her own boundaries millennia ago.

Egan sighed.

They were finally on their way back to Faerie.

What they would find there was a mystery.

Probably that nothing had changed. In a couple thousand years.

The plane boarded and the five of them were sitting close, he and Skye together. Glenna and Pearce directly behind them. Adaire was across the aisle from him. He got on after the others. As he went to sit down, he noticed Adaire's pale face.

"Are you okay?"

"I'll be fine. I just don't like flying."

He nodded and sat down, stuffing his backpack beneath the seat in front of him. He'd given Skye the window seat. As if he could keep her away from it. Her eager face was glued to the window.

Egan stood and got a blanket from the compartment above him. He spread it over him and turned the fans above his seat towards Skye.

She turned and smiled at him, then returned her gaze to the window.

"I do believe you'd fly all the way there if it was safe."

"Of course I would," she said.

Egan settled in and waited until the plane took off. He chose not to watch the movie. Some boring cop thing. He got a coffee from the cart that came by. And a small bottle of whiskey that he poured into the coffee. He drank it, which made him all warm and cozy.

He slept through the rest of the flight, waking only when the plane touched down in Galway.

It didn't take them long to move through the airport. They'd only brought their backpacks and would get rid of them soon. Soon they would be in their Fae bodies with no need for human clothes.

Just outside the terminal, Adaire pointed at the newspaper stands. The headlines were all about an offshore earthquake and tsunami. And major flooding on the west coast, especially near Limerick. There were missing fishing boats. And entire towns flooded, people dead.

Pearce bought a paper and they read it. There didn't seem to be any logical reason why the flooding had gone so far inland in that area. The port was declared a disaster area and the Shannon was inundated with strange sea creatures washed up by the tsunami.

He grieved for the loss of life. Humans were so fragile, they lived such short lives anyway, that each one dead was such a loss. The Fomorians must have been responsible. How could they have gotten here so quickly?

They'd decided to stay in human forms and not use magic unless they had to. The earthquake and tsunami seemed like the Fomorians' work. Were they trying to attack Faerie?

Or had they been following the others, Dylan, Meredith and Lynette? He wondered how far they'd gotten. Were they still out at sea or had they made it to Faerie?

Whatever the answer, they decided the Fomorians were a bigger threat than humans, so they'd better play it safe. It seemed apparent that the Fomorians tracked them easily when they were in their Fae bodies. Why, they didn't know.

Perhaps it was their glow. All Fae glowed. The glow was greatly diminished by wrapping themselves in human bodies.

And to dampen that glow in their Fae form took a lot of energy. They needed to save that energy because they might greatly need their magic later.

For all they knew Faerie might be surrounded by Fomorians.

They left the airport and made their way down the road, passing through the town of Shannon. Past the whitewashed, stone and brick storefronts of the older part of town. They blended in, looking like tourists. As soon as they could, the five of them headed off to the northeast, away from the city. Away from the roads.

Following the old paths, the grassy fields soon turned to brush and even a few trees. They followed hedgerows where ever possible, trying to remain unseen without using their magic.

Egan was enjoying the heat of the sunlight warming his skin, even if he had to stay in a human body.

They kept walking until long after dark, passing through wildish areas when they could. Smelling the sweetness of elder flowers and crabapple blossoms. The trees outside of Faerie had changed since Egan had been here last. There were more evergreens here. Planted in straight rows as if they were being farmed.

They moved through long grassy, weedy fields and scrubby woodlands of birch and willow, which followed a stream he had no name for. They finally stopped to sleep in an old abandoned barn. Their human bodies needed rest.

Another day should take them to Faerie and all they had were questions.

Chapter 25 ✦ Balor

Balor stood on the wrecked deck of a ship. All that was left was the metal flooring beneath the decking and an upright post with the sail on it. It made a nice raft, just large enough for his feet to stand on and his arms to grab onto.

He was drenched with seawater, not a comfortable situation for a god of drought to be in. But necessary. He'd suffered worse.

Inundated by the smell of fish and water, he longed for heat. The hot sun and the smells of baking soil and crispy dried out plants. All he could taste was salt.

Conand, of the North wind, had blown him eastward across the Atlantic. Dela, of the South wind, summoned up a hurricane to aid in the speed. Domnu pushed her waves, making his raft move faster. He'd been on this boat for nearly a day, but he wasn't tired. He was a god. Gods didn't tire easily.

He'd waited so very long for this.

Land was finally in sight. Cethlenn waited for him. As did Corb and Elatha, he knew. He hoped they'd gathered a few others.

By now Faerie would know they were coming.

He smiled beneath the gray clouded sky as his raft hit the rocks and he leapt off. His bare feet scrambled on the stony beach, crushing limpets beneath them, his toes grabbing the slippery kelp.

He looked at the dozen or so of his people standing on the shore.

This was going to be very satisfying.

War.

They were finally going back to war to take back their land.

Chapter 26 · Fiachna

Fiachna found a fifth desecrated grave. The large boulders tossed aside, as if by giants rolling balls. The Luminary's bleached bones tossed aside like trash.

He sank onto one of the hard stones. The smell of unwashed bodies and shit still lingered in the air.

He had spent millennia walking the borders. Making sure Faerie was protected. And he was weary.

Fiachna took out his leather water skin and sipped fresh, clean water, splashing a bit of the coldness on his face.

It was time to end this. He needed to rejoin the world of the living. To rejoin the life of Faerie. He'd grieved long enough.

He'd punished himself for far too long.

And this needed to be addressed. He had to see for himself. Make sure the Luminary understood. That the boundaries around Faerie were continually being unraveled. By their enemies.

No one had responded to his previous messages. No one had sent more boundary keepers.

Fiachna smelled the same deep earthy smell that had been at the other tombs. It was as if the earth herself had opened up and broken apart the stones forming the barrow.

White night moths hiding in the shadows fluttered away as he used his magic to move the boulders, rebuilding the barrow. Then he collected the scattered bones, laying them on the stone slab inside. Once, woven cloth had lain beneath the bones, it had long rotted away. He collected soft green moss, making a layer of that upon which he placed the bones.

As he worked tears slid down his wrinkled face. He'd known this Luminary. A strong, yet compassionate man whose tomb didn't deserve this desecration.

Fiachna picked some of the blue trumpet flowers and the yellow marsh marigolds and laid them amongst the bones.

"I am sorry, my Luminary. Your current successor is not worthy to be on your throne. Trouble is coming and I fear he will not be up to facing it. He has grown soft with the many years of peace. I must go warn him."

His decision made, Fiachna sealed up the tomb and threaded the boundaries around the boulders, making them strong. He pushed his energy through the fringes of Faerie, trying to close the edges as far down the line as possible. He could feel there were more breaks, farther down. But he needed to go back inside. To make sure his messages had been heard.

A raven croaked at him, perched in a nearby tree.

Fiachna shook his head, "Not today my friend. I have no need of you. I must go myself. You may go look for whatever interests you."

The raven flew off towards the nearby road.

His mouth felt dry as if filled with sand.

It wouldn't be good if humans stumbled in through the open boundaries. Humans and Faerie had never mixed well.

But it couldn't be helped.

Fiachna slipped through the boundary like a pebble falls into a stream. He made small ripples in the energy field and moved into the lushness that was Faerie.

Except that the edges weren't lush anymore. It was as if the magic had leaked out where it was unravelled.

He walked for an hour or two before he came to the Faerie he'd once known.

Fiachna had to remove his cloak as he walked towards the center. It was much warmer inside the boundaries.

Inside Faerie was vast, much larger than the outside. It would take him a day or two to get there.

Bees hummed amongst the everblooming flowers: nasturtiums and bee balm, oregano and lemon balm. The insects, heavy with pollen, lifted off and flew towards their hives, brimming over with honey.

Fields of wine grape vines dripped with heavy, ripe fruit. Planted nearby, luscious strawberries were ready to pick. He could smell the sweet berries' perfume just walking by.

Faerie was a feast for the senses and he'd starved himself for far too long. Punished himself because she chose another over him. And he couldn't stand to see them together.

He didn't know if they were even still alive. Or if it mattered. His love for her had faded with the millennia of tending the boundaries.

Down the road walked three warriors. Warriors had always existed in Faerie. Younger Fae who needed an outlet for their energy. And who trained relentlessly in case of war. Mostly they were stone and fire Fae.

Their bronze armor glistened in the warm sunlight. Their swords were sheathed and they were passing a wine skin between them.

He tried to pass by them, not meeting their eyes.

"Boundary Keeper, why are you here? Why are you not outside?" asked a tall, earth spirit.

"I've sent messages. I need help. I need to warn the Luminary."

"Warn him about what?" asked the cocky young fire spirit.

"The boundaries are being broken. The barrows opened."

"It's those pesky humans. Treasure hunters," said a short, dark stone Fae.

Fiachna shook his head. "No. Not human. Much older. One of our ancient enemies."

"Who?" asked the rock spirit.

"The Fomorians."

"That's not possible, they're all dead," said the fire Fae. "You worry too much old one."

Fiachna shook his head. "You underestimate them. One can't kill a god. They are alive. Immortal. And waiting for the right moment to strike."

"That can't be," said the tall earth spirit.

"Why don't you go outside and walk the boundaries? Talk to the stones of the ruined barrows? They'll tell you what is happening. Or are you afraid to leave the safety of Faerie?"

"I'm not afraid. You just go give the Luminary your message. We'll go guard the boundaries," said the stone spirit.

"Good. I've repaired this one. There are more broken places. You'll see."

Fiachna kept walking. He didn't believe they'd actually go outside. But he hoped they would.

Faerie had been isolated from the world for far too long.

Chapter 27 ❧ Adaire

Adaire walked through the knee high grass and heather, basking in the sun. It was still early spring and a little cool out. Having lived in Seattle so long she'd gotten into the habit of sucking up the sunlight whenever it appeared, just like the resident humans there.

She'd missed the warmth and heat so much.

The heather flowers were filled with noisy, happy bees and she was careful not too disturb them. A slight breeze blew across the hillside, carrying the faint smell of blooming crabapple trees. She sipped on her water bottle, trying to keep her human body happy. Who knew how long she'd need to stay in this shell? They'd been searching for Faerie now for two days.

It was close. But they couldn't find the exact point to pass through. And they didn't want to abandon their human bodies until the last second before they entered.

The whole area reeked of Fomorians.

She recognized their smell by now. Whether they were ocean, wind, fog or something else, they carried a peculiar, elemental smell. There was almost a metallic tang to their scent.

The boundaries of Faerie were tricky. If you were human and unaware of the boundary, you just walked through it, not noticing, and never entered Faerie. It existed within the spaces of the human world.

It was very difficult to find the entrance in a human body. Human senses were so dull, no matter how one enhanced them with magical powers.

To enter Faerie one must be fully in their senses and consciously seeking the edges, even for the Fae. Humans could only enter by invitation. Fomorians never.

At least she hoped that was true.

"I give up," said Egan, sitting down on a boulder at the edge of a great pile of them.

Skye had long ago given up. She stood looking longingly up at the sky, watching the clouds float past.

Adaire walked up to the spot where Egan had given up. She closed her eyes and held her hands out in front of her.

She could hear the bees buzzing, feel the sun on her back. Feel the dizziness of activity in the world.

Then after a few minutes, she picked up a hint of the radiance of Faerie. It was close. She shuffled forward a couple of steps, her eyes still closed. There. There it was. They'd walked through the place several times already, not recognizing it.

She shed her human body, letting it drop into the heather, which sucked the form up as if it had never been. Interesting. She hadn't caught that this variety was a Faerie plant.

All that was left behind were the clothes and her daypack.

Then she motioned to the others and stepped through the invisible wall.

Adaire was completely inundated with her senses. She felt as if they'd been dead for years and had just now reawakened.

The luscious smells of roses, jasmine and millions of bluebells filled her nose and spread throughout her body, loosening the tension. The sounds of hundreds of songbirds singing in harmony with each other, punctuated by little silver bells hung in the trees came to her ears and filled her with ecstasy.

The earth felt moist and spongy beneath her bare feet. Trees whispered of the return of a dryad.

Nearby a small stream sang with joy. Adaire squatted down on the soft, lime green moss bank and dipped a hand in the stream, wetting her mouth.

It was the cleanest water she'd ever tasted and just a handful completely quenched her thirst.

The air around her body felt humid and earthy.

She stood and began walking, watching the others. Egan, Skye, Pearce and Glenna were entranced by coming home as well.

Adaire found a path that moved towards the center of Faerie and followed it, her body flowing, almost dancing.

Roses lined the path. Not the hybrid teas of humans. These were ancient roses, sweet fragrant roses. Tall wild dog roses and others, that humans named Gallica or Apothecary roses. Single petaled, pink to ruby to purple colored. Their perfume surrounded her almost as if she could see and touch it. Rambling white and pink roses climbed high into the surrounding trees, their scent flooding the air. Despite all the trees, there was enough sunlight for all the understory plants.

Hydrangeas sat behind the roses, their plump pink and purple blooms adding to the lushness. Flowering vines: Clematis, passionfruit and honeysuckles wove through the shrubs and up into the trees. There were flowers everywhere.

And there were exotic flowers that hadn't been given to humans. Flowers which when given to another gave part of one's heart and soul. Flowers, the scent of which could inflame lust or the desire to kill. Flowers to eat, flowers which would heal a broken heart or could break one of a Fae's choosing. None of these plants had names. Fae didn't have the burning passion to label everything that humans did. So often a plant's uses were lost in the mists of time. Some of this was just as well.

A plant's uses could always be rediscovered, mostly by earth Fae.

It was nearly always summer in Faerie. Closing it with an energy field must also trap the heat in. Or perhaps the magic of Faerie changed the climate. She remembered snow as a child.

And the trees, they were as magnificent as she remembered. Hollies, oaks and yews, some as thick as ten people bundled together. Ancient wrinkled and sagging trees as well as young flexible saplings.

She sighed deeply and tears of joy came to her eyes.

As the others followed her along the path, she saw one of the purple Gallica rose bushes lose all its petals in a puff of breeze. The petals came to life and floated through the air above their heads.

The rose petals preceded them into the heart of Faerie, as if carrying a message. But what message?

Adaire continued down the path, which gradually widened. She and the others passed through fields of glorious fruit and vegetables, grains and hives of bees.

Earth spirits tended the fields, harvesting the bounty of Faerie and caring for the plants.

Farther on, others were making wine from grapes and apples.

They walked until the sun went down and the waxing moon rose. A small blue-green lake lay in front of them and they decided to rest. It had been a long trek to get here.

Adaire was so very weary. It would take some time before her Fae body recovered from being encased in the human body and being held prisoner, so close to so much cold iron. She shivered at the thought and pushed it away.

She curled up in a mossy hollow at the base of an ancient oak tree. Safe, finally. The tree sighed at her as she lay down, pleased to be near a dryad. Adaire felt as if she were finally home. She just wished all that was required would be to care for the trees.

She watched the others lie down to rest. Egan slept on a boulder which still held the heat of the sun. Glenna and Pearce slept near another boulder, on the soft grass. Skye lay stretched out on the grass, face down with her head propped up on her hands, on the low bank overlooking the lake. The moon and sky were reflected in the smooth water.

Adaire dozed, but her dreams were filled with dark, threatening Fomorians.

Monsters attacking Faerie.

Chapter 28 ·◈· Meredith

Meredith sat on a lichen covered rock overlooking the valley below. The land was divided up by stone fences and hedgerows planted to make roughly square or rectangular fields. The fields were being grazed by sheep, cattle and horses. She could smell the animal dung even up high on the hill.

Small houses seemed to have been built next to most of the fields. It was a lovely pastoral scene, which would have made a pretty painting. One which she hadn't seen for a thousand years or so.

It hadn't changed much. Except that now power lines were strung to each of the houses. There were vehicles parked near many of them. Colorful paint decorated many of the little homes, others were painted a stark white making them stand out from the green fields.

Dylan sat on a nearby rock. He looked out at the valley, an expression of sadness on his face.

The rock she sat on felt lumpy and Meredith shifted her body and closed her eyes. She was exhausted. She'd used up too much of her magic with no chance to recharge. They'd run from the very water which could have recharged them. Because Domnu controlled it. She would have crushed them if she'd caught them.

They'd been walking for what seemed like forever. Through grass and heather and white wildflowers which all seemed to be out celebrating spring. Her feet were raw from all the rocks and human roads they'd walked on. They'd travelled mostly at night, so they could remain unseen by humans. They wore human bodies, but had no clothes.

Dylan wasn't as tired and she'd let him lead.

But he couldn't sense Faerie.

He had no idea where it lay, however much he said he did.

She brought her attention back inside herself and went deeper, trying to find a part of her that had enough energy, enough magic left to find Faerie. Through the thick, dullness of this human body she wore.

It was a shoddy job she'd done, making this body. It was done much too quickly. And on the run.

There was no breeze at the moment. She couldn't sense any Fomorians at least.

Meredith slipped out of the human body, letting it slump down onto the rock. She stood and let her senses find Faerie. Her energy reached out in front of them, searching. Looking for that special vibration. The field behind which lay Faerie.

Finally, her energy travelled far enough to sense it.

They were still a ways away. Faerie lay quite a ways past the valley. Over towards the rocky hills in the distance. In that copse of trees.

She pointed and said, "There. Faerie lies over there. In those trees over those hills."

Meredith slipped the human body back on. She felt slightly rejuvenated. They were close.

They rested all day, hidden among the stones. She worked on healing her feet, making them tougher. They darkened their skins, made their night vision better. Improved the weak human bodies they'd made so quickly. Meredith slept on the grass, communing with the water contained within the plants, trying to recover her magic.

At dusk they made a run for it.

They ran past the brightly lit homes. People inside gathered around their TVs and computers. Humans. They spent far too much time in front of screens. They'd always been seduced by the hunt. The hunt for what they might find elsewhere. Rarely satisfied with what was before them. Always in search of the next best thing. What did their screens find for them?

The moon rose in the sky. Only a half moon, waxing. It didn't provide a great deal of light, but their night vision was now better. They'd planned for this.

On the other side of the valley ran a narrow, cold stream. They paused there, sucking up as much energy as they could from it, waiting until the breathing of their human bodies returned to normal.

The water tasted sweet and clean, moistening the mouth of the much abused body she'd made.

As they moved across the rest of the valley, she could hear the squeaky cries of curlews feeding in the grasslands. White night moths fluttered among the wildflowers.

They ran up into the rocky hill beyond. Finally, they had to slow down. They picked their way up the hillside, finding a trail and following it to the top.

Then beyond that hill lay another, and another.

They crested the last hill before the thicket of trees and shrubbery. Dark shapes moved below them and Meredith squatted among the stones, quickly pulling Dylan down with her.

They watched the giants below. Tearing apart a barrow. The sod covering the mound flew off as the boulders were thrown. Some cracked on impact, after hitting other rocks.

There were three giants.

Fomorians.

When they'd finished tearing the top off and opening at least one of the sides, they went down inside the grave and threw bones around, scattering the grave goods. They picked up some of the jewelry, holding the shiny pieces up to the light of the moon and slipped them into their baggy pants pockets.

They wore no shirts or shoes and their torn old pants were obviously made for oversized men. The bottoms of the legs came up to just below the giants' knees.

Monsters.

Then they finally left.

After it felt safe, Meredith and Dylan climbed down the rocky hillside. The air stank from the Fomorians.

They circled around the broken barrow. Meredith shook her head. What they'd done was terrible. Anger and the feeling of violation built up deep inside her, churning in her belly.

How could Faerie allow this to happen?

This was no time to linger. The Fomorians clearly had no one to challenge them here. There was no telling if more might come along of if the first group might return.

It was then she realized the extent of their actions.

The barrow had anchored the boundary to Faerie.

Now it floated loose.

Anyone could walk right in.

Had the monsters even known what they'd done? Was it intentional?

A stream ran down the hillside and into Faerie. She slipped out of the human body and made it dissolve. Then she became a salmon again and swam into Faerie.

She glanced at Dylan, who'd done the same. Once inside, she did what she could to anchor the boundary.

It helped a bit, but she felt a greater unravelling in the edges. There were more loose places.

She couldn't fix all of them. Her magic hadn't recharged enough.

They needed to tell the Luminary. If there was still a Ruler. Or someone in charge.

She hadn't been here for a thousand years.

Who knew what had happened in that time?

Everything could have.

Or nothing.

She was hoping it wasn't the latter.

Chapter 29 ⚬ Egan

The next morning Egan woke on top of a boulder, stiff and cold. He heard the others moving about.

Skye was flying over the lake. Twisting, turning and doing somersaults. She giggled and screeched gleefully. Pearce and Glenna were sucking on reeds, probably drinking the sweet nectar. They seemed more whole and energetic than he'd ever seen them. Adaire stood embracing a tree, a look of bliss on her face.

Egan stood and walked into a stream of sunlight. It wasn't terribly warm, at least not yet. He needed some clothes to keep him warm. He'd find some when they reached the center of Faerie. Here in the outskirts, he probably wouldn't find much.

Fae didn't tend to wear much clothing. Except for ornamentation. But fire spirits away from the fire were always cold.

Once he was up, the others began to gather and head down the trail. The others probably couldn't really sense well where the heart of Faerie lay. He knew they were distracted by the trees or the rocks. But the big fires which drew him in were at the center of Faerie. They burned in his consciousness and he knew exactly where they were.

Skye couldn't fly very often without leaving them all behind, unless she went high over the tree tops. But when they came to fields and open areas, she took to the air and zipped around, playing tag with birds and chase with dragonflies.

They walked for what must have been hours before coming to the first real village. Before that they'd seen only single dwellings off by themselves. Some Fae wanted to live in solitude. Most Fae were much more communal. Most of the buildings here were made of carved wood.

Egan warmed himself by a blaze built for firing pottery. He gloried in the heat, but didn't climb in, not wanting to damage the pieces being fired.

This village was for artists. There were metal workers, potters, painters, sculptors and all manner of creative people. Most of them worked outside or in buildings with open walls. He generally loved seeing the rampant creativity that all Fae possessed. But here were the ones who had devoted centuries to their work.

A female fire spirit who was roasting hot peppers caught his eye. She was lean with yellow and red scales on her back that extended over her shoulders and down the tops of her arms. It had been a very long time since he'd seen another fire spirit and he couldn't take his eyes off her.

The peppers in Faerie were so hot they made the humans' 'Carolina Reaper' peppers feel like yogurt.

She smiled at him and offered him one. He took the steaming hot pepper and popped it in his mouth.

"You look cold and weak," she said, her face crinkling in sympathy.

"I've been cold for the longest time," he said, chewing the pepper. The oblong red fruit made his mouth scream

with heat, but he let it pass over him. He could feel the
pepper spreading warmth throughout his body. Burning.
Making him feel alive again.

When was the last time he'd felt warm from the inside?
The heat made him tingle as all his nerve endings came
awake again. He could feel the magic of the pepper doing
its work.

He could feel everything.

He smiled at her, "That was wonderful."

He reveled in the aftertaste of the pepper, rich, full and
smoky.

She wrapped several of them up in a huge leaf, folding
it over and over so they wouldn't leak. Then put them into
a small leather bag with a long strap and gave it to him. He
put the strap over his head and one shoulder, wearing the
bag across his body. He bowed to her.

"Eat one several times a day, until you feel warmer."

"Thank you."

"It's my pleasure. The peppers long to be shared and
appreciated."

Egan smiled at her. He would have loved to stay and
get to know her. He would have liked to learn pepper lore.

But they had to keep moving.

Perhaps he'd come back some day.

They kept walking through more villages until they
came to the outskirts of the center of Faerie.

Here the buildings were older and more formal. They
were built of carved stone. The finest Fae stonemasons
who'd spent many millennia learning their craft had built
them. The color of the stones varied between white, yellows,
grays, reds, greens and even blue shades. Every now and
then they passed a building which had been completely
painted by an artist. Woodland scenes were the most
common, but some were covered with underwater scenes
and even the occasional fire scene.

Entire worlds were contained within fires that most Fae
couldn't even imagine.

Unlike human inner cities, nature abounded here. Each of the buildings had courtyards and fountains and elaborate gardens where plants were encouraged to go wild.

Trees towered throughout the center of Faerie, so old their expansive growth would have taken up blocks in a human city. Vines were allowed to ramble up the walls outside buildings and enter inside.

There was no need of windows to enclose the buildings, although occasionally intricately designed stained glass filled entire panels.

Here there was no need to keep nature out. Faerie lived in harmony with nature.

The streets of Faerie were lined with large greenish stone pavers. Horses, cows, goats and pigs tended to stay in the grassy fields along side the walkways. The fields were unfenced, large and plentiful.

Streams crisscrossed the city with fresh water to drink. Water plants grew in and alongside the creeks, filtering the water, shading fish, frogs and salamanders. There were bridges which crossed the streams, but also places to easily wade right in. The water in Faerie was always immaculately clean and tasted like no water from anywhere else he'd ever been.

Birds of all colors and sizes flitted among the trees and bushes. He didn't know their names. Croaking, chirruping and cooing filled the air around him. Squirrels, deer and martens wandered through. As did badgers and hares. The city was filled with life.

Best of all were the smells of Faerie.

Roses, jasmine and gardenia, mingled with strawberries and fresh milked cream. Peppers combined with smoked trout. There was no end to the wonderful scents filling the air.

His mouth watered from the smells.

As they walked, he unwrapped the peppers and ate another one. His mouth singed from its heat. He began to feel whole again. As if he'd been lost for a very long time. Some of the darkness which hovered around the edges of his heart and mind dissipated.

It seemed to take forever to get to the center. The buildings became grander and more ornate. Every section carved. They met more Fae on the streets, parading along in a rainbow of silks and gauzy fabrics. Wearing large amounts of gold or silver. Their long hair braided into styles which spoke of large amounts of leisure time.

Gatherings of Fae lay around listening to musicians or dining on the most succulent scented food he'd ever smelled. Even a few making love in public.

Fae had such different rules for propriety than humans did.

And it seemed that things in Faerie hadn't changed in the thousands of years he'd been gone.

Would their news make anything change?

By the time they reached the Palace, the sun was setting and the moon had already risen. The nightbirds began their slow deep songs. Frogs called for mates.

The Luminary wouldn't see them until morning. The Court would be reveling.

They chose to spend the night in a meadow. Skye flew high up in a tree and perched there. Glenna, Pearce and Adaire slept beneath various trees.

Egan looked longingly at the nearby fires. These were flax or sunflower oil fires. They burned hot and steady.

Finally, he said, "I'm going into the fire. Call me in the morning if I'm not back.

Adaire nodded, sleepily.

Egan walked toward the fire and hung his leather pouch on a sculpture, marking it as his own by making his forefinger burn a fire symbol into the leather. He hadn't been able to do that in a very long time.

Then he walked into the fire and curled up to sleep. Warm and loose, relaxed at last.

Chapter 30 ❦ Balor

Balor paced the ground outside Faerie, his heavy footfalls shaking the earth, causing boulders to roll down the hillside.

He smiled, his ancient grin missing a few teeth.

They were ready.

The boundaries had begun to loosen. A few humans had slipped in, accidentally, so his people would need to move quickly. Before the humans' presence was discovered. Otherwise the Fae would probably discover the loosened boundaries and his people would have to begin all over again.

On the West side, the first in was Cethlenn. Flowing with her fog past the edges of Faerie like the cold fingers of death. Creating cover for the others, which included Domnu, her deep waters flooding the land.

On the East side went Elatha and his small band. On the North came Corb blowing in like a tornado, destroying everything in his path.

Balor's side was the South.

He removed the layers of bandanas from his head. Stuffed them in the front pocket of his baggy pants. He crept beneath the loosened boundary. Once inside his third eye opened.

He gave his baleful glare to a tree. Heat poured out of his third eye, streaming towards the ancient holly tree. The furrowed bark dried up and cracked open, exposing the softer skin inside. Which opened up in turn. The liquid inside the massive trunk dried up as the tree died. Nearby shrubs withered and shriveled. Some of them dried out so much they caught fire.

Everywhere his eye touched fire and drought burned through the land and famine would follow. Behind him were his troops, ready to kill whatever survived his gaze.

He smiled. He hadn't lost his touch.

The Fae would be exterminated.

The land would belong to the Fomorians again. Then they'd wipe out those pesky humans.

He was hungry for the smell of charred flesh.

Charred Fae flesh.

Chapter 31 ⋘ Fiachna

Fiachna had taken the fastest route to the city. He'd asked a sturdy looking, white mare for her help and she consented to carry him. He stood on a boulder and swung up on her back, holding onto a hunk of her mane. She ran all the way to the city, only stopping once for some water.

He slid off down on the road in front of the Palace and bowed. The shining white palace sat high on the hills above him.

Fiachna turned to the horse, thanking her.

"It was my pleasure to carry you," she said to his mind, then bowed to him and went over to a grassy field to roll in some sweet grass.

Fiachna's legs felt like rubber, he hadn't ridden in a very long time. His pants were wet from the sweat of the mare.

The sun had just passed midday as he climbed the tall and wide outdoor stairs to the grand entrance of the building. Now the palace was formed from rows of tall white barked trees. Their trunks arching at the top of the building, growing together at the top and forming a canopy.

Once inside the massive carved wooden doors in front, the black veined white marble floor felt cool and smooth to his rough bare feet. He felt a little shabby in his torn clothes and his dirty cape, but his news couldn't wait for him to bathe and find nice clothes.

He walked down the long hallway. Inside it was formed of tall stone arches open to the sky. The throne room where the Luminary interacted with his people sat at the end of the hall.

There was a long line. A Court Official came up to him. She was tall, her long red hair, even braided, hung past her knees. She wore the purple and gold sash which marked her as a servant of the Court.

"What is your business with the Luminary?"

"I'm a Boundary Keeper. Perhaps the only one. The boundaries around Faerie are being opened. I keep closing them, but the Fomorians are following along behind, opening them. I can't keep up. I sent messengers, but there's been no response. We are open for attack."

"The Fomorians? They're long dead."

"No. They're not. They're alive and about to attack us."

"Perhaps you need to rest."

"Perhaps you need to send someone to look at the boundaries and find the Fomorians who are tearing apart the barrow mounds. I've found ten desecrated graves already. I know there are more. And I'm old enough to know what Fomorians smell like. To recognize their magic. They're alive and Faerie has been opened."

The official still looked skeptical, but she called for a couple of air spirits. The air Fae listened to what she had to say and ran out of the building. He could see them taking flight as soon as they left the palace.

Fiachna stood in line, waiting, for what seemed like an eternity. The Luminary sat on his throne, listening attentively to each person. Asking a few questions and then making some sort of decision.

He was a big Fae. Tall and well muscled. Rumor had it that he had been a warrior in ancient days and that he still practiced with weapons.

His long dark hair was twined into multiple plaits and those were woven together until they all came together in one thick braid. He wore the purple, trimmed with gold, flowing pants of his office, leaving his chest bare. Around his waist was a leather belt with a sheathed long knife. Other than a gold tie for his braid, he wore no ornamentation. His feet were bare at the moment. Leather sandals kicked off.

The Luminary looked like a powerful ruler for all his casualness. And the people who Fiachna watched treated him so.

But he was too casual. He hadn't answered Fiachna's messages. Hadn't taken them seriously.

He'd left Faerie undefended.

And over the last two thousand years Fae had been leaving Faerie. Unwilling to withdraw from the outside world. To watch Faerie's retreat. Some of the most powerful had left and never returned.

He shook his head.

A flurry of activity as five air spirits landed and ran to the Highest Official, who stood near the Luminary.

They spoke to the official. Fiachna watched as his eyes widened. Fae didn't often express fear, but the High Official looked like he wanted to flee.

Instead he turned to the Fae speaking to the Luminary, and held up his hand signaling him to stop.

The Official whispered in the Luminary's ear. The Luminary stood, spouting orders for his warriors to gather.

The Luminary looked at Fiachna and waved him up. Then he put his hand on the shoulder of the Fae whose long story he'd been listening to, "I must interrupt our conversation."

The Luminary stared at Fiachna.

Fiachna made his way up through the crowd, who parted for him.

The Luminary glared at him. "Why did you not come earlier?"

"I sent two previous messages, days ago. Ravens brought them. I received no response, so I came myself. Did you not receive the messages? About the Fomorians?"

"Fomorians, they're all dead. Well, it is too late now. All the boundaries are open. We're under attack. Who is it?"

"It is the Fomorians. You can't kill the old Gods. They simply faded for a time. Now they're back and opening all our borders."

"If we can't kill them, how can we defeat them?" asked the Luminary.

Fiachna stared at him, open mouthed.

It was then that five tall Fae came into the room. He could feel their power, fresh and strong. They'd been out in the world. He could feel the influence of the world on their energy. They were alive in a way the Fae who lived in Faerie weren't any more. And they smelled different. Like a fresh spring wind filled with rain. Like sunlight on warm skin. Like the pungent scent of daisies.

He stepped back to let them speak.

Chapter 32 ⋅☙⋅ Adaire

Adaire felt the great age of the trees which made up
the supports of the palace. They rose up three stories tall.
Hawthorns and fastigated yews, rowan and ash. The palace
smelled earthy and old. There was a stuffiness in the air, like
in a room closed up for too long with many people in it.
The air wanted to freshen itself.

She had a vague recollection of the palace as a living
being. That changed itself from time to time, according
to the Luminary or outside events. Perhaps by its own
whim. Sometimes it looked different to different people.
Presenting itself as what the viewer needed to see.

It seemed in need of a change.

High above the colonnade of trees the branches, leaves
and needles grew together to form a tall, arched living
ceiling. Birds flitted in and out, squirrels and other small
creatures jumped from limb to limb.

In between the supports vines had woven themselves
thick enough to form walls. Boulders, polished by years of

attention, sat in a semicircle around a large throne, carved from the roots of an overturned, dead oak tree. Behind the throne lay a large pool of water, fed by a stream.

Upon the gnarled throne of roots sat the Luminary. It wasn't the same one as when she'd left, that one had been a female air Fae. A sylph, like Skye. This Luminary was an earth spirit. He was a reed spirit.

Why had he been chosen as leader?

Surely, he must be too weak. Reeds were flexible, but weak compared to other spirits.

Egan wove his way to the front. She and the others followed.

The Court felt chaotic. Something was going on. More panicked Fae were filing into the hall every minute.

She could feel tension, confusion and fear growing in the room.

Egan stood in front of the Luminary, the fire spirit's arms folded and flames leaking from his body. No one had acknowledged their presence, except a Fae standing off to the side. He was older and smelled of rocks and earth. His magic was stronger than most. He bowed and stared at them as if waiting for something to happen. For them to act.

No one else met their eyes.

Adaire sent a message to Glenna and Pearce. They nodded and focused their attention on the vines of the palace walls, helping them untwine. Letting them make spaces between the pillars of trees, allowing fresh air to blow through the palace.

She watched Egan. He was about ready to explode with anger. The peppers he'd been eating had brought his power on full force. Adaire could hardly stand next to him, he radiated so much heat. She felt like he would burn her up.

Finally, she said in a loud, deeply grounded voice which shook the earth around her, "You must listen to us."

Everyone turned and looked in surprise. Seeing them as if for the first time.

The tree canopy rustled and dead leaves and twigs fell from above. The dust that came with them glistened in the sunlight, like pieces of crystalline rainbows.

"Who are you?" asked the Luminary, standing.

The five of them gave their names.

Adaire was last.

"I am Adaire. The five of us, and many others, left Faerie over a thousand years ago. We weren't willing to shut ourselves off from the world. We've been living with humans, as humans, in different parts of the world. Until recently, when we and many others were captured. By the Fomorians, the old gods. Most of the captured Fae have perished. Only the five of us and three others escaped."

She paused and stared at the Luminary.

He asked, "How can I believe such a story? The Fomorians are dead. There is no way they can be alive. It must be humans who are responsible."

Adaire felt furious. Was he too afraid to take charge? He seemed afraid of losing face, but more than his appearance of competency would be lost if he didn't.

Egan burst into flame and moved closer to the Luminary.

"We have seen them. We were kept captive in their cold iron boxes," he said.

The Luminary shivered, his face blanching white as a birch tree.

Egan continued, his body still flaming, "It took all of us to escape and to elude their pursuit. They are coming. They intend to destroy Faerie and exterminate all of us. You must wake up and act or you will be the Luminary who allowed our old enemies to wipe us off the face of the Earth."

Adaire shivered. She'd never realized Egan could draw on such power.

Behind the throne, three figures rose out of the water. Water Fae transforming from fish. Scales changed into the pale skin of water spirits. Fins grew into arms and legs. They stepped out of the pool.

When they'd finished, Adaire recognized Meredith, Dylan and Lynette.

She smiled. They'd made it across the ocean safely. She'd been worried about them.

The Luminary noticed people staring and turned to face the pool. Adaire watched his back and shoulders tighten. His entire body became rigid.

With what? Fear? Anger?

She couldn't tell.

Chapter 33 ⚬ Meredith

Meredith shook off the water and pushed back her long greenish hair. She stepped from the palace pool and stood on the sacred ground that was the heart of Faerie. For the first time in over a thousand years, she was home.

The throne room was a sea green color. Kelp dripped from stone arches imbedded with the mother of pearl sheen of shells. The room smelled of fish and salt, making her feel at home. The back of the throne looked like a lion fish carved from stone, spines sticking out everywhere. It was glorious and regal.

Dylan and Lynette, now found, dear child, stood at her back, adding their considerable power to hers.

The room was about half full of Fae and in front of the throne stood the Luminary.

Meredith hid her surprise.

She hadn't expected it to be him.

She gazed at the Luminary, meeting his eyes.

Challenging him.

It was the only way.

He shook with anger. He knew what the challenge meant.

Then he recovered, rather quicker than she expected.

At least he'd learned something in a thousand years.

He nodded, acknowledging her.

"Varion," she said.

"Meredith."

"I see the others have arrived. They have told you of the Fomorians."

"I do not believe it."

"You always were a fool, little brother. You will believe it when they come to kill you. And the rest of us."

"You cannot insult me like that. I am the Luminary now."

"Yes, I see you standing by the throne. Doing nothing to counter this attack. They are making war on us, they've entered Faerie and you sit flapping your lips."

He bristled.

It really was too easy to insult him.

And it served no purpose.

"I've been told they can't be killed. How to fight such an enemy?"

She sighed, exasperated.

"You must outwit them. Trick them. They need to be confined somewhere. Permanently." She was thinking on the fly. He wouldn't, couldn't come up with a plan. She had to.

Her brother's face wrinkled up, as if he was puzzled.

"You must act! Now! Or all of Faerie will be destroyed!" roared Egan.

Meredith jumped, startled.

She'd sensed his power when they'd first met, but it had increased tenfold on his return to Faerie. Her brother's power had decreased since she'd left.

She said, "Varion. Wake up."

He shook his head, "I don't know what to do. I don't know how to outwit them. I'm not powerful enough."

"I will tell you, but you must make the sacrifice. You must lure them down to the vaults."

"I suppose there's no other way," he said, his face drooping. She remembered him doing that as a child.

Just before he betrayed her.

As he always did.

"Open the vaults!" yelled Egan.

Several officials looked at Varion. He nodded, a look of despair on his face.

Everyone moved out of the palace to the stone courtyard in front. Meredith, Dylan, Lynette, Adaire and the others moved towards the front. Following Varion and his officials.

Fae were bringing huge oxen and hitching them to rings set into metal doors on the other side of the courtyard. The teams of oxen pulled open the metal doors, along with spiraling, ostentatious magic done by the Court Officials. More for show than any actual power.

Where had all their power gone?

Meredith remembered the only time she'd seen the vaults opened. It was when Faerie had been closed, just before she'd left it. Faerie's most precious treasures had been put there for safekeeping. To mark the center of Faerie. And to anchor all the boundaries.

It was tied in to the boundaries. What effect would opening it have?

The sword of Nuada, the cauldron of Dagda, the spear of Lugh, the stone of Fal. All these, plus golden chalices, gemstones set in gold and silver. Much of the art their people had made. The physical and spiritual wealth of their people, lay down in that vault.

The heavy doors wrenched open with a metallic croaking sound which was so loud it echoed through the courtyard. Cold air rushed out, along with the smell of earth. The walls and floor of the vault had been lined with perfectly cut stone and solidly mortared to keep water out. The sun hit the treasures lying in the open pit and Meredith was nearly blinded by the shimmering light, hidden for so long.

"Come, let us remove our treasures," said Varion.

"No!" said Meredith. "It must stay. Otherwise the Fomorians will not take us seriously."

"Surely, the Four should be removed," said Varion.

"The Four especially must stay. They are our power. They will help keep the Fomorians confined," said Meredith. "Now, go down the stairs and choose a few minor things to remove."

He did as she said, beckoning some of his advisors to go with him.

They descended the stairs into the pit and began looking through the treasures. Occasionally, one of them brought something up, an ornate torc or a jeweled knife. Something worth saving.

Meredith noticed she was steaming and turned to find Egan standing very close.

"Control yourself," she said.

"He will try to escape."

"Of course he will. We must keep him in. He will wait till the last minute. Right before the door closes," she said.

Meredith watched as her brother and the officials wove beneath the massive metal and stone columns which had been built to support the heavy metal doors. The Vaults were deep. If they heaped a mountain of stone on top, then perhaps, just perhaps… With spells in place. It might hold the Fomorians.

Meredith turned to one of the stone spirits standing nearby, "We must get enough large blocks and boulders to seal the top. Can you and your kind have them standing by? Our spells will only hold them alone for so long."

He nodded and bowed at her.

"I will see it done." He turned and left, gathering his kind as he left.

The cold wind blew and the fog came, shutting out the sun.

The first Fomorians had arrived.

Chapter 34 ❧ Skye

When she sensed the Fomorians, Skye fled, flying up on top on a tall stone building that overlooked the courtyard. She knew their winds could knock her off in a second. Toss her in the air like a seed.

Still, she felt safer there than on the ground.

How could this plan work? It seemed impossible to contain the gods. One of them, she didn't know which one, made earthquakes. How could they contain that in a simple deep pit?

Of course Fae had different magic than that of the Fomorians. Perhaps Meredith knew some sort of binding spell that would disable them.

Skye certainly hoped so.

She felt the winds, Conand and Elatha, and the fog, Cethlenn, move into the pit. She struggled to hold on to the top of the building, their power drew her to them. Perhaps far back, they were even kin.

They were obviously drawn to the power of Faerie.

They must have recognized the Four. Those items in particular had caused the Fomorians' downfall if the Fae's old stories were to be believed.

Then came Corb, of the sea, and Domnu, the deep abyss of the ocean. They had transformed themselves into humanlike bodies, but their wateriness couldn't quite hold the forms.

There were others whose real names Skye didn't know. Earthquake, deluge, tsunami.

Last of all came Balor, drought. His gaze burned a path in front of him, leaving the white stones of the courtyard with a scorched, deep black trail. Then he closed his third eye and put kerchiefs on to hide it.

Skye noticed when Balor saw the Luminary down in the pit, with all the others. Varion wielded Lugh's spear and Nuada's sword, trying to do as much damage to the Fomorians as he could. Some of the court officials had also found swords as well.

She watched as Balor saw the Four. The sword, the spear, the cauldron and the stone.

He too was drawn to them.

Sucked under by their power.

The history and mythology of the Fae was contained in the four treasures. It was impossible to believe they were going to be lost forever.

There was something else there too. She felt as if Meredith had added a little extra something to the Four. Even Skye could feel the longing to possess them, as if they contained everything she'd ever wanted.

As the giant Balor plodded down the great stairs, the earth shook beneath his feet. He wrenched the sword of Nuada from Varion and held it high. Yelling out in victory. The Luminary huddled near the foot of the stairs, still holding the spear.

A cone of magic spiraled out from Meredith's hands. She joined with Adaire and Egan. Skye felt herself drawn into the spiral. Her energy was sucked into a dome which Meredith was creating over the vaults. The elder water spirit was drawing power from Egan, Adaire, Dylan and any other Fae near her.

Skye's power was at Meredith's disposal, but her mind reeled at what the elder was doing. Skye had only heard about Fae using other's power. Never had she witnessed it. It was the stuff of the old stories, from when Fae were young.

She had had no idea Meredith carried that much magic. Or that she could withstand using all the energy flowing through her.

Meredith had been using that reservoir of their power to gather up the energy used in maintaining Faerie's boundary, building on the enormous power she held until it reached a peak. She had unraveled the boundary completely, reeling the magic in, transmuting it and using it to seal the vault. Entrapping the Fomorians.

And her own brother, as well as three court officials.

Skye felt grief for the Fae. And a sort of relief, mingled with disbelief, at the Fomorians' capture.

Then the heavy doors were being pushed back into place. The earth rumbled as the Fomorians understood what was happening. Some of them ran for the stairs.

The Luminary was there first. He tried to get up the stairs and escape, but was knocked backwards as he hit Meredith's spell.

As soon as the doors were slammed shut and sealed, much quicker and easier than they'd been opened, massive stones were floated over the top and set in place by hundreds of stone Fae. Granite after marble after white quartz.

The earth continued to shake. Water tried to flow out, but was contained by the spell.

Skye could feel the air, the winds trying to escape. They too were powerless against Meredith's spell.

Meredith continued to draw on the power of others. Skye watched as she kept a balance of earth, air, fire and water, using whoever was nearby. Fae were streaming into the courtyard as if called, and allowing their power to be used to maintain the spell. Those who had already helped and were exhausted, left the center, moving to the edges so they could keep watching.

Skye watched as two nearby buildings were dismantled and the blocks floated over by Stone Fae. After several layers, they began to form a ring of stones. Mortaring everything in place. Sealing it. Water spirits, then it filled with water.

Soil was brought in, by earth Fae and around the ring, copper panels were placed here and there. Roses and vines were planted, their stems wrapping around the panels, clamoring up them. Water lilies and lotus were put in the pond by sprites and undines. As were orange and yellow fish whose shiny scales glistened in the sunlight.

A stone island was created in the center of the pond. One of the large metal bowls was set in the center and an oil fire was lit. It would burn forever.

Skye flew down to the tiny flame and blew on it. The flame leapt higher. She'd added air to seal the spell, completing earth, water and fire.

Then she landed near the others. She felt so weary and worn out. Still her mind reeled at Meredith's ingenuity, flexibility and strength.

When the spell was finished, Meredith collapsed. Dylan caught her before she hit the ground.

Chapter 35 ⚬ Fiachna

Fiachna wearily followed the others into the palace. He was exhausted and covered with dust from prying loose blocks off nearby buildings. And placing them over the Vault.

His magic felt depleted.

He wanted nothing more than to go sit in the woods, by a quiet stream. Drinking the sweet water and allowing his mind to join with a pile of stones. To soak up their energy.

So, he reveled in the coolness of the palace, feeling the energy of the surrounding stones begin to fill him up again. The beautiful green chalcedony pillars of the colonnade, the marble floor, swirling in black and white. The floor felt smooth beneath his feet. The throne made from strands of gold, copper and silver which had been woven together, sat empty.

The palace smelled charred.

The Luminary was dead.

Or dying in the Vault.

He had seen the necessity of it. Still, Fiachna felt they had committed a terrible crime.

The Luminary had been chosen by Faerie. By the land, the water, the air surrounding them and by fire. Yet, Meredith had probably been right. None of them had seen another way to contain the Fomorians.

They lay Meredith on a low platform off to the side of the throne room. Water Fae huddled nearby, the young undine stroked Meredith's face, moving her wild hair off of it.

Fiachna knew they were trying to infuse her with their power.

It wouldn't work.

He'd seen it happen once or twice in his long life. Fae who used up all their power. Held nothing back. It had always been for a good cause, but once the power was drained so low, there was nothing that could be done.

If she lived, she'd be powerless.

To be a Fae without power must be an awful thing.

But she'd saved all of them.

And perhaps the world.

Because after they'd destroyed Faerie, Fiachna had no doubt that the Fomorians would have turned their attention to the humans. They had little reverence for the living.

Fiachna could feel the unease of everyone present. They were leaderless and the boundaries of Faerie had collapsed. Someone needed to take hold.

He walked over to the fire Fae. The strong one who'd been outside Faerie.

"What's your name?"

"What?" asked the fire spirit, looking away from Meredith and towards Fiachna with confusion filled eyes.

"I asked you your name."

"Egan. Why?"

He clearly was preoccupied with Meredith.

"Because someone needs to take control here."

"Meredith…"

"Will be damaged. If she lives. She will be without any power. She used too much of her own power to save us. Don't make her sacrifice count for nothing. There are several Fae over there, from the old court, who are just waiting to take power. They will be as inept a leader as Varion was."

"I know nothing about the court. I've been gone for a thousand years."

"Good. We need strength and we need new ideas. Faerie has been growing weak for too long. It should never have been closed off from the world and those in power stayed too long. This Earth, and humans, need us to help them. Now, go up to the throne and speak. Claim it as your own. You might be challenged. I think you can deal with that."

Egan stared at him.

Fiachna could almost see the thoughts spinning his head.

Egan stroked the leather bag which hung at his hip and turned to walk up to the throne. He stood in front of it and fire blazed from him, creating a corona.

Everyone turned to look at him, drawn by his heat and magnetism.

"My friends, we must act. The boundaries of Faerie have been thrown wide open. We will probably never again have the power to close Faerie completely. I have spent the last thousand years among humans. They are a good people, although a bit paranoid. We must mask our world for a short time. Let them discover us gradually. To do otherwise would invite war. We must teach them to live with us, to live with this Earth and not destroy it."

"No! We should have nothing to do with humans," said

one of the former court officials.

"How do you propose keeping us secret?" asked Egan.

"I agree with Egan," said one of the newcomers. The powerful dryad. She stood close to him, although not so close as to catch fire. The woman had long dark hair and skin the color of pale oak leaves. She was lean and muscled.

"I too have lived among the humans. They need guidance or they will destroy this world. They've been left on their own too long and like errant children, need to be tutored and directed towards healing the damage they've caused. They desperately need our help."

One of the newcomers, a water spirit, stood up beside Egan as well. He said, "I agree. Water is the life blood of this Earth. If we do not cleanse it, their filth will infect our water as well. With the boundaries of Faerie gone, our water will mingle with theirs. We must enter into their world more fully. But quietly at first. Choosing those able listen without fear."

The group of court officials began to drift away from each other. None of them had the magical power to directly challenge Egan, even without his supporters. They had no plan. They couldn't put Faerie back together again.

An old fire spirit standing next to Fiachna said, "It's been a very long time since a fire spirit was the Luminary. A very long time."

"I call for a decision," said the sylph who was part of their group. She hovered above the arched ceiling above the throne.

"I add my call to hers," said Fiachna.

"But we don't have another choice," said one of the court officials.

"Do we need one?" asked Fiachna. "When Nuada was reinstalled as Luminary, a second choice was not needed. When Lugh was given the task, a second choice was not needed. Sometimes the answer is clear. As always, the elements will decide."

Finally, one by one, the Fae in the room took up the call.

And the elements answered. The throne turned to flaming metal. The colonnade gained an aura of fire. The pool behind the throne gave off a halo of rainbow colored flames. A breeze blew through the palace making the blazes flare. For a few moments, the entire palace became an inferno. Just long enough to make a point.

Then the flames waned. The dryad next to Egan looked rather faint. The water Fae looked dried out.

Egan's intensity would be difficult for some.

Ravens were sent to speak with every Fae within Faerie.

Fae warriors were stationed by the vault. Everyone knew it was just a matter of time before the Fomorians broke out. Hopefully, the vault would hold them long enough that another solution could be found.

By the time the sun set and the moon rose, Egan was declared the Luminary in an official ceremony.

He sent earth, water and air Fae to the old boundaries to make them look impassable.

Fiachna chose not to go.

Just this once.

He felt weary of protecting the boundaries.

Chapter 36 ❦ Egan

Egan stood in one of the humid palace baths where Meredith lay propped up against a stone wall, inside a pool which was fed from a sacred well. Her skin was a pale green, but since he'd mostly seen her in human form or in distress, he didn't know for sure what she really looked like. Except she looked sick and in pain. He smelled seaweed and fish.

The room was tiled with royal blue, turquoise and cream colored smooth tiles. Inset into them and forming curving patterns were a variety of beautiful shells. Water musically flowed down the walls like a pleasant stream deep in the woods. Light filtered into the warm room through a frosted Fae glass window of a green blue color.

The light made the room feel like it was underwater. At least to him. Who had never once been underwater. and never intended to be. Fire Fae were cleansed by heat and sand, not water. Water merely dampened their fire, or put it out. Sometimes permanently.

Even being in the steam made him uncomfortable. His body just expended more heat to keep him dry.

He removed a piece of one of the peppers from the leather pouch and nibbled on it, feeling the burning in his mouth and the back of his throat. The sweet peppery taste danced on his tongue. He closed his eyes for a couple seconds, enjoying the sensation. Feeling the fire hit his body and energize it.

Egan shifted from one foot to the other, watching Dylan, Lynette and three other water spirits tend to Meredith. One of them was always feeding her energy, as if it would reanimate her.

He wasn't sure it would.

The room changed. The water rolling down the walls turned quickly into steam which crept beneath his scales. It felt uncomfortable, even though he like the heat.

The palace made him feel uneasy. It kept shifting wherever he walked. As if responding to his presence, making a place for him that was the most conducive to fire spirits wherever he went. But to do that was to exclude many Fae who couldn't be comfortable in the heat.

He didn't want that.

Egan scratched a scaly arm.

Two days had passed and Meredith still wasn't awake. She was alive though. That was something.

He felt torn between coming up with a plan for helping Faerie integrate itself into the rest of the world and staying by Meredith's bedside.

Dylan rose from Meredith's side and motioned for Egan to follow him out of the room. They stood in a wide corridor made of red marble.

"You need to leave. You're not helping her heal," said Dylan.

"I don't know what else to do," admitted Egan.

"You're turning the place into a sauna. She needs coolness."

Egan looked at Dylan, "I did that?"

Dylan nodded his head and sighed. "The palace is responding to you, mostly. Normally, it changes depending on who is viewing it, everyone sees the palace they expect and are comfortable in. Who knows what it actually looks like or is? But now it's overwhelmingly reacting to you, no matter what anyone else wants to see. Look, we'll call you the moment she becomes conscious. Don't you have work to do?"

"I do. But I'm worried about her."

"We all are," said Dylan. "But the best healers in Faerie are here. If they can't help, certainly you can't either. Go focus on what only you can do. Work off some of your heat."

Egan nodded and left the water Fae to their work of tending Meredith.

Most of the old court officials had left the palace. Many of them were plant or water spirits and felt uncomfortable around him. But that left the normal palace routine in complete disarray.

He knew no one here and trusted them even less.

Except the rock spirit, the older one, Fiachna. He was solid.

Egan knew other advisors would come, but he needed advice now.

He climbed up the stone staircases each step flaming higher until he found himself on the roof. It seemed like the more he panicked about not knowing what to do, the more heat the environment around him produced.

Nine reservoirs of oil were spaced out between stone benches. Fires blazed away on them, the flames whipped around by the breeze. Several sandpits had appeared on the roof. Egan removed the leather pouch and set it on one of the stone benches.

He stepped over a short stone wall and into the sand. Then squatted and began rubbing sand over his skin and scales, scrubbing himself clean.

The sun blasted down from above. It felt hot.

Several fire spirits were clustered around the center of the roof, basking in the heat. Sleeping.

He didn't want to wake any of them. They probably weren't who he needed to talk to. Most fire spirits cared little about court politics.

After Egan had cleansed himself, he put the leather bag back on and walked around the back edge of the roof and sat down, crosslegged, leaning his back against a reservoir. He closed his eyes and went deep inside himself.

Throughout his body ran channels of fire. They were leaking terribly. He attempted to thicken the conduits, but as soon as he patched one area, another sprang a leak. There was simply too much energy to handle.

He needed help.

Egan got up and walked around the perimeter of the roof, looking downward at the land he was suddenly responsible for.

He found Skye crouched on the front edge of the roof, overlooking the buried vault with a worried look on her face. The wind blew strong up here.

He asked, "When you're inside the palace, what do you see?"

She looked at him, a strange expression on her face.

"When we first came it was a meadow with a stream running through it. Tall trees on all sides. The breeze danced between the leaves, making them flutter. Butterflies and birds floated on the zephyrs. Then when you were confirmed as the Luminary, it changed. Now, wherever you are, it's stone and fire. When you're not around, it's still stone. All the other elements become present now and then, but it's as if water and plant life feel uncomfortable. They can't breathe around you."

"That's what I've sensed," he said. "I don't want it to be like that. I've lived too much of my life where there was no fire around and it's painful. I don't want others to suffer the loss of their elements."

"Perhaps it's just a temporary deprivation for them. Maybe it's what they need, to feel the loss, so they can understand what it's like. Because that's what's facing the Earth if we can't get humans to help take care of her."

"Perhaps. I need your help," he said.

"I'm sorry I haven't been around. I'm worried about them," she said, pointing to the buried Vault. "I don't see how it can hold them. Even beneath all those rocks I can hear the winds, trying to break free. They won't give up you know."

"I know. It was Meredith's strategy, but none of us had any other ideas. It's bought us some time though."

"What do you want help with?" she asked.

"Do you remember when we came to Faerie? The village we stopped at where I got the hot peppers?"

"I remember."

"Could you find the female fire spirit? The one who gave them to me. And ask her to come here?"

"I think so. If she'll appear to me. Fire spirits are tricky, sometimes they only appear to other fire spirits."

"I know. Try, please. I'd go myself, but I need to be here. Coming up with a plan to help us move out into the human world."

"I'll go. It won't take long. Then, I'll come back and help. Talk to Adaire. She'll help you. And find a water spirit to join in the conversation. I think that's what went wrong when the decision was made to close Faerie. Not all the elements were consulted. We need balance. We need people who've been out in the world, who understand humans."

"I agree. That's why the changes in the palace worry me. I don't want it to be a place that excludes water and earth spirits."

She nodded and flew off the top of the building, heading in the direction they'd come from when they entered Faerie.

He felt the flapping of her wings as a small breeze which momentarily fanned his flames. He needed to talk to other fire spirits. To learn how to control himself better. Being away from Faerie and away from real fire, he'd lost the knack. It was as if, in a thousand years he'd forgotten everything he'd learned as a child.

Chapter 37 ⚬ Adaire

Adaire stood amongst a grove of ancient oaks near the palace. The earth felt cool and moist beneath her feet, although the mosses were drying out. They needed some rain. It hadn't rained in Faerie in the two days since Egan had been chosen. Normally, it rained every night for a short time.

Still, nearby roses were blooming, their scent perfumed the air. The sound of working bees made a constant buzzing sound. Water sprites floundered around in a small lake down the hill. A diminishing lake, but a lake nonetheless.

Adaire touched the grooved bark of her beloved oak trees. She was finally home again. After a thousand years.

It didn't feel like home.

It felt as if all of the water in Faerie was focused on healing Meredith. The plants cried out for water.

The land had been neglected. The pools were drying out. The streams running low. Water Fae were growing pale and sickly.

Adaire had no ideas for a cure.

Meredith needed to live.

Even if she was now powerless as many said would happen.

The trees grieved for her loss. Adaire hoped it was worth it, hoped the Fomorians would be contained. Forever.

But that seemed unlikely.

Glenna and Pearce seemed to have disappeared into the woodland somewhere. She hadn't seen them since the day Egan became Luminary. They must have gone off to heal themselves. They'd never talked about their time as prisoners of the Fomorians. In those cold iron boxes.

Adaire shivered.

Lynette and Dylan were closeted in with several other water Fae, trying to heal Meredith. Skye was off by herself. Egan was busy burning up the world.

Adaire actually felt lonely.

And useless.

After a thousand years living as a human, she'd caught the human need to be doing something. To work.

And yet, there was nothing for her to do here. She couldn't make water come to the trees and other plants. If this was a human garden, she'd set up an irrigation system. And water. But water in Faerie was becoming scarce.

She was hoping she wouldn't have to resort to setting up a watering system. Faerie was vast. It would be difficult to cover that much land. But she would to save her beloved trees.

She had no answers and wandered beneath the trees, trying to will them back to health. Her feet cushioned by the soft moss which was growing crunchier by the day. Even the breeze blowing through the grove felt dry and the smell of damp earth she'd always associated with the place had turned to smoke. Everywhere near the palace smelled smoky these days.

Was Faerie burning?

Or was it the Fomorians, come up with a way to escape?

She left the grove and tiptoed along the hot stones of the walkways. The pavers hadn't felt hot when the five of them had arrived.

Adaire made her way to the palace. She decided the best way to find Egan was to follow the heat. She passed through the throne room, the colonnade of trees, now withered and turned to stone. The throne which had been made of tree roots was blackened rock. The pool beyond, which Meredith had appeared out of, was a circle made of smooth, carved obsidian. Now it was filled with flames.

She found Meredith in a bathing room. Nothing had changed.

Dylan held up his hands in helplessness, looking at Adaire with a strained look on his pale face. Lynette sat, holding Meredith's hand, tears streaming down her cheeks. Two other water Fae, who must be healers considering the knotted strands of seaweed they wore around their necks, sat by Meredith's head and feet. Adaire could feel the energy flowing through Meredith. It was as if they were keeping her blood flowing. Or perhaps her water.

Adaire left the room. She sought the heat and found it centered on the roof. Egan sat on one corner of the roof, the wind fanning his flames.

He was black and red, his body had almost completely covered itself with scales and he had an aura of fire. Except it wasn't really an aura. It was him.

"Hi," she said. "Can you turn down the heat a little? I need to talk to you."

"That's the problem," he said. "I can't turn it down. I don't remember how."

"You need help."

"Yes, I do. I've sent Skye to get someone. At least I hope she'll be able to help."

"What's your backup plan?" Adaire asked.

191

"I don't have one."

"You need one."

"I can't think clearly anymore. It feels I'm just beginning my life. Everything I've ever known is gone. I can't even control the smallest thing and I used to own a cafe employing a hundred people. Now I can't even regulate my temperature. It's as if my brain is burning up."

"Have you been eating or drinking?"

She watched him think.

"Uh, I ate most of those peppers. Before we talked to the Luminary. I only have half of one left and don't remember when I last drank something."

"Eat something. Drink something. I don't know if it'll help, but even Fae bodies need nourishment and you're running explosive amounts of energy. I'd guess you need more than a normal Fae."

He nodded. "Any other advice?"

"Don't fire spirits have elders or healers?"

"Not very many. We tend to be loners. That's why I had Skye go find the woman who gave me peppers and ask her to come. She has some knowledge. Of peppers at least."

"Was it the peppers that made you lose control?"

"No. I don't think so. They healed me. Brought me back to life. I think it was becoming the Luminary. Faerie has filled me with power that I don't know how to control. Yet," he said.

"Well, the trees are feeling the heat, as are the rest of the plants. They're drying out, parched, blistering. We need some rain. I'm feeling the heat. It's painful to be near you. I can't stay much longer. I need coolness and dampness. It feels as if all the water in Faerie is being used to heal Meredith."

"I know. I wish I could do something. About Meredith, and my lack of control. I will get this taken care of. Soon."

A blast of wind preceded Skye's arrival.

She was panting and flapping her wings.

"That felt great!" she said.

"Flying?" asked Adaire.

"Yes. I haven't been flying enough. I've been worried about the Fomorians, Meredith, and Egan."

"Is she coming?" asked Egan.

"Yes. She said you need to closet yourself away till she gets here. Find a room of stone, with a pool of water. Sit in it until the water's sizzled away. Then add more water. And keep doing that."

Egan's face scrunched up.

"That sounds counterproductive," he said.

"That's what she told me. She was already packing when I found her. She knew there was a problem," said Skye.

"What have you got to lose?" asked Adaire.

"All my power," said Egan.

"That would be bad," said Skye. "But so would the death of Faerie. Let's get going."

The three of them stood and went towards the nearest stairwell. Adaire stayed well behind them, away from his heat.

On the main floor they found an empty bathing room with a fountain and pool in it. Egan went inside. The room changed its colors from lavender and white to an icy gray blue when he entered.

"Call us if you need more water," said Skye.

Adaire and Skye went a ways down the hallway and sat on the nearly cool black tile floor. As far from the heat as they could be, but still within shouting distance.

"Do you think it'll work?" asked Adaire.

"I don't know. I don't quite understand the problem. But his energy's way off."

"He says he can't control it."

"That's pretty obvious," said Skye. "When I was pretending to be a human, I worked as a healer. I did a lot of energy work. Every now and then, I'd come across someone who needed an excess of what was wrong with them for their body to find balance. Then there were other people who needed the opposite of what their problem was. Sometimes it's hard to tell. Lassair, that's her name, seems to know what he needs. I sure hope so."

They stayed there all night, occasionally checking on Egan and getting others involved to help carry water to fill up the pool.

Finally, Skye kicked Adaire out because she became so overheated her long black hair was singeing.

Shocked, because she hadn't even smelled it, Adaire left the palace.

She retreated to the lake below the oak trees. She fell asleep with her feet in the too warm water.

Chapter 38 · Fiachna

Fiachna was helping move heavy wooden buckets of water to fill the pool. The fountain in Egan's bathing room had stopped working. The water refusing to go where asked.

Stone Fae were earth spirits who could handle the heat. The fire spirits couldn't handle the water. The water spirits were all fading and couldn't even come near Egan. But the stone Fae were strong.

Fiachna moved four large buckets, floating them along and keeping them level so as not to spill. He entered the bath. The room was steamy and smoky at the same time.

Lassair arrived with another fire spirit. A very young Fae. Skye accompanied them, fanning her wings to clear the hot steam out a window.

Her actions helped Fiachna see the pool again. It was almost dry. He set the buckets on the floor and began pouring the first one in. As soon as the water from the buckets hit the tiled pool, it began to sizzle and turn to steam.

Fiachna's mouth felt dry. The heat was affecting even him. He bent down for another bucket.

Fae young were few. Since Fae lived such long lives they didn't have many offspring in order not to outgrow the land. Even Faerie had limits.

The pool kept drying out. As the water hit Egan, it turned to steam.

"Oh dear," said Lassair. "It's not working, is it?"

Egan said, "I don't know."

Skye said, "He seems confused."

Lassair said, "Step out of the water."

Egan did and was almost instantly dry.

Lassair walked around him and turned to Fiachna, as he emptied another heavy bucket of water into the pool.

"Do you remember how long it's been since a fire spirit has been the Luminary? It hasn't happened in my lifetime."

"Not since long before Faerie was closed. We've only had three Luminaries in the last thousand years. Water, air and lastly earth."

"Can someone tell me what happened the day he became Luminary?"

Skye told her all that had happened; Egan's night spent in the fire, the encounter with Varion, Meredith's arrival and the burying of Varion, the three court officials and the Fomorians. Then Faerie's acceptance of Egan as the new Luminary.

Lassair said nothing.

"Mama, I know what's wrong," said the young one.

"What dear?"

"He has air, water and earth running through him. I can see them. They're cutting holes in him."

Lassair stared harder at Egan, then touched his hands and closed her eyes.

"Aine's right," said Lassair. "Somehow with the spell, he absorbed the other three elements and wasn't able to slough them off. He's carrying them and they're killing him."

"How do we remove the other elements?" asked Skye.

"We need a water spirit. One who's very strong and can handle a little fire. And you for air and you," she said, pointing at Fiachna, "for earth. And we need to do a cleansing ceremony. Now, or we'll need a new Luminary soon."

Skye said, "I'll go find the water spirit."

She fled from the room.

Fiachna stood watching Egan. He looked weak, but was still spouting flames.

It wasn't long before Skye returned with Dylan. He looked tired.

Would he even be able to complete the ceremony?

Lassair said, "You, stand in the water."

Dylan didn't argue.

"You stand by the window."

Skye went over to the open window.

"You," she said pointing to Fiachna, "lean against that stone wall."

Lassair moved Egan so that he was in the center.

She asked Aine to stand outside the open doorway and keep anyone from coming in.

Lassair placed herself in the fourth corner.

"I want each of you to ground yourself in your own element. Feel the fullness of it. Revel in the touches, the smells, the sounds, the tastes, the different ways it can look. The vibrations of its energy."

Fiachna lost himself in the earth. Rich, moist soil. The feeling of cool, hard rock. The salty taste of rocks by the sea. The sounds of rocks growing and moving. The beauty of mottled jasper and ornate marble. The heaviness of iron, the lightness of gold. The high energy of the metals compared to the languor of sandstone The changing light of opal.

He could feel it when Lassair touched him with her energy. She drew a line of power between him and Egan. Turned it into a tube. Fiachna could feel her drawing out the earth energy from Egan and transferring it down the tube into himself.

In response Fiachna's energy created a suction. Kept the energy flowing into him. After a time, she finished with him and made the tube and line disappear.

Fiachna grounded the excess energy, sending it down through his feet, through the stones in the palace and down to the earth beneath the floor. He felt the earth receive it and transfer the extra energy to the bedrocks beneath the palace.

It felt pleasant to give back to the Earth in that way.

He opened his eyes and stood quietly, feeling full and content. Watching Lassair do the same to Skye. Dylan stood in the fountain, trying to get his strength back so he could withstand his turn.

Fiachna could tell when Lassair finished with Skye. She looked lighter, as if a puff of wind would blow her out the window like a cottonwood seed.

The sylph was smiling. She probably felt the same way Fiachna had, giving her excess energy to the breeze.

Lassair turned to Dylan.

Fiachna could tell when she made contact with him. Dylan stiffened, as if bracing for a blow. Then he relaxed a bit, allowed the energy to flow into him.

After a time it looked like he would burst with joy.

Fiachna guessed that most of the foreign energy that Egan had received during the spell gone wrong had been water. Meredith had been one of the most powerful Fae long before she left Faerie. She could have been a Luminary had she not been opposed to closing Faerie. Hers wasn't a popular view at the time. Perhaps it still wasn't, but that point was already decided.

It took much longer to extract the water from Egan than the other elements.

Egan was no longer blazing, instead he looked tired. As one should after a long battle.

Finally, it was done. Lassair broke off contact with Dylan and sank down onto the floor. Her daughter ran into the room and stood watching her, to make sure she was okay. Lassair waved at her, a gesture which Fiachna took to mean that she was fine, she just needed time.

Dylan was glowing, almost bursting with energy.

"I must go see Meredith, give her some of this back," he said. Then he ran from the room.

Egan stood in the middle of the room, looking lost.

"Come on, my Luminary. Let's get you to the roof," said Fiachna.

He took Egan's arm and slowly led him to the roof of the palace.

Lassair and Aine followed. Skye flew out the window.

Chapter 39 ⚭ Dylan

Dylan ran into the blue and white tiled room where
Meredith lay in the pool. Lynette and the two healers who
sat with her looked up at him in surprise.

He knelt at Meredith's side in the warm pool water.
Nothing had changed. Her consciousness was far away, it
was as if she was sleeping at the bottom of the lake. Except
that her energy still felt drained.

The wall had turned itself into a gentle waterfall. Ferns
grew out of crevices in the wall and around the pool. Moss
was beginning to take over the floor.

Dylan noticed the water had grown cooler since he was
last here. Egan's healing must have had an effect.

He felt alive, juicy and vibrant. He could smell moisture
in the air, taste it even. The sunlight which streamed in
the window looked a little less harsh. The plants growing
outside the openings in the wall looked a bit greener, less
washed out. His senses were keener.

The water energy which had flowed out of Egan had been overwhelmingly Meredith's.

Dylan didn't question how or why that had happened.

He touched Meredith's arm and felt her energy flowing inside him. It felt like he simply opened the valve and poured Meredith's power back into her. She struggled at first, as if wanting to let go of her life. But he couldn't allow that, not if he had any power to change it. She needed to be here. She still had things to do in Faerie.

Finally, she allowed the magic to flow back into herself. Perhaps accepting that her life wasn't over yet.

Meredith's color deepened to normal. Her breathing slowed and no matter what else happened, whether she lived or died, Dylan felt somehow as if Faerie had come back into balance. All of the elements were back in place and in harmony again.

The fresh water in the pool cooled down more. The other water Fae in the room looked more healthy.

Dylan sat back and took a deep breath, for the first time in days. He hadn't realized how badly he'd felt. How he'd been burning up.

Now, he felt whole again.

Meredith's eyes fluttered open. She took his hand, squeezed it and smiled. Then she closed her eyes and went back to sleep.

One of the healers said, "She's resting now. She'll heal and then we'll see what damage has been done."

The other healer nodded. "Why don't you two leave? Go swim in the lake or walk in a stream. Come back when you've rested."

Lynette nodded and silently left the room. Egan knew she was going to the lake. To see her family. She hadn't gone to see them since she'd been back.

He stood and left the room. Then he walked out of the palace, not knowing where to go or what to do. He felt as if overflowing with energy.

Dylan hadn't been anywhere since he'd returned to
Faerie. He'd followed Meredith into the palace and then
stood by while she dealt with her brother and then the
Fomorians. Then he'd tended to her for the last few days.
He'd been back in Faerie for three, maybe four days and so
much had happened, it seemed like weeks, maybe months.
In Faerie, time was always slippery.

But finally, he was free.

He walked through the formal gardens, letting the
energy leak away, providing water for the parched plants.
Moistened soil stuck to his damp feet. He continued on to
the forest walking through groves of oak, rowan, holly and
ash trees, walking over the gnarled, exposed roots of the
ancient trees.

He waded through a nearly dried-out creek, watching
the waterside primroses perk up as cool water percolated
up through the stream bed. The water level rose until it was
full.

Frogs began to croak and splash in the water. Doves
flew down and bathed in the shallow spots, cooing at each
other in pleasure. Dylan sat down in the stream, watching
them. Trout swam around him and he felt their scaly bodies
slip and slide past his bare skin. Rain began to sputter
lightly and then it poured down for a few minutes until
everything in Faerie felt bright, fresh and clean.

His senses reveled in all that was Faerie. It was good to
be home again.

He dozed off in the stream, hanging onto a tree root as
an anchor.

When he woke it was two days later.

And it was a human who woke him.

Chapter 40 ❧ Meredith

Meredith opened her eyes. She was lying inside the palace, on a pool shelf, her head resting on a stone pillow, her feet hanging off the shelf and in the deeper water. The water smelled fresh and felt cool. Clean.

A waterfall spilled down one wall, whispering its secrets to her. Something about summer coming.

Two water healers sat on the white and blue tile edged pool, their legs and feet in the water.

Why were they here?

Then she remembered.

The Fomorians. And how she'd buried them and her own foolish brother with his cronies. Alive. And the spell had gone wrong. She'd been too weak to channel it all. And Egan had become so very powerful, clearly Faerie's favorite candidate for Luminary, even before Varion was dead.

Towards the end of the spell, all the power she'd been harnessing ended up flowing into him, instead of it being grounded as she'd intended.

Meredith managed to rasp out, "Egan. How is he?"

"He's fine now. Don't you worry about him. It's you we need to make sure about," said the elder of the two.

"What do you mean by 'now'?"

The younger water healer sighed and said, "Skye found a fire healer and she was able to heal the Luminary. He's been asleep for two days, but he seems better now. He nearly burned up all of Faerie."

"How are you feeling?" asked the elder healer.

"I think I'm fine." Meredith felt chilled from the water. She managed to sit up and touched her feet down on the bottom of the pool. She moved over towards the side and got out, sitting on the edge of the pool, off to the side of the two of them.

Someone had brushed and braided her wild hair, interweaving and binding the multiple braids with the striped leaves of reeds and strings of pearls. Her mother had done that for her when she was a child. What an act of kindness. It had probably been Lynette.

She did feel well, but something was missing.

She couldn't feel much connection to Faerie. Couldn't feel the water energy and she had no ability to affect anything.

Her magic was gone.

Sadness filled her heart. An aching emptiness grew or perhaps it had been there all along, lurking like an octopus, waiting for its prey to swim by. She felt alone for the first time in her life.

In the heart of connection, she was alone.

And vulnerable.

The healers brought her raw salmon and the finest red dulse to eat. She ate, tasting not the intricacies of the flavor, only the salt.

All her senses had been dulled.

Was this what it was like to be human?

Then it hit her. She probably couldn't breathe underwater, that's why they'd placed her on the shelf, instead of submerging her in the pool. She'd never again swim the deeps of the ocean.

Meredith began to sob, her body shaking with the grief. The loss of everything she loved.

The healers moved closer, sat on each side of her and held her while she cried.

After a time, the tears ended.

"I'm sorry," Meredith said. She even sounded like a human.

"It's to be expected," said the elder.

"I feel so weak."

"It was a grand sacrifice you made," said the other.

"The Fomorians…"

"Are still contained. We've seen no sign of the spell you created weakening. And there are Fae who've chosen to stand guard permanently."

"What about the boundaries of Faerie?" asked Meredith. "They've all been opened."

"We'll leave that to the Luminary, now that he's up and about. I'm sure he'll do fine taking care of it. Our work is to make sure you're healed."

"I think your work is done then," said Meredith, standing.

They stood with her.

"You're sure you're feeling well?"

"To the best of my being able to sense."

"Well, call for us if you need help. Don't overdo it, you were seriously injured. It was only Dylan pouring all your energy back into you that saved you."

"Dylan. Where is he?"

"After he finished healing you, we told him and Lynette to go rest. They hadn't left your side since the spell went wrong."

_dded and said, "Thank you for all you've
me. I'll call if I need help. Please, go rest. I'll
_ find Egan. The Luminary."
_e smiled.

That was something to be grateful for. He'd make a fine
Luminary. Strong.

She walked down the warm stone hallway.

Perhaps she didn't mind the warmth so much anymore.
The magic may have been taken from her with the spell.
She might even need to wear clothes to keep her warm.

Part of her held out a small hope that her magic would
return, with time.

Egan was in the throne room, sitting on a stone bench.
A fire burned nearby. He was speaking with Skye, Adaire, a
male elder of the stone spirits, who looked vaguely familiar,
and two other fire spirits, a woman and a young girl.

He rose when he spotted her.

"Meredith! Should you be up walking around?" he
asked.

"I'm fine. Well, I have no power, but I'm well."

"Come, sit down with us," said Adaire, patting the stone
next to her.

The room felt warm and comfortable to her. The scent
of smoke lingered in the air as the wind changed direction.
On a grill above the fire, peppers were roasting. The smell
made her mouth water, although she knew from experience
they would be too hot for her. Never eat the hot peppers in
Faerie. She'd learned that lesson as a child.

Meredith sat down.

After the introductions and pleasantries were done, she
said, "Now, what do you plan to do about the boundaries of
Faerie being destroyed?"

Chapter 41 ·☙· Skye

Skye sat on a hard crystalline chair in the throne room, her arms wrapped around her knees. She tried to ignore the conversation going on.

The west wind blew in between marble pillars and tall oak trees, whispering to her of the movement of corncrakes, the flight of fritillaries and dancing of damselflies.

She longed to be out flying. But not alone.

And she was alone.

The air spirits who served the palace had left. Angry about the sacrifice of the last Luminary, who they'd been in loyal to. She'd tried to talk to them, but they wouldn't listen.

Other sylphs had gone to explore now that the boundaries were down. Searching for any renegade Fomorians.

No others had come to take their place.

She was the only air spirit, the only sylph, for miles around.

And oddly enough, she missed being human and the company of humans.

She only half listened to Egan talk about what he thought should be done about the boundaries.

"I think we should send Fae, disguised as humans back out into the human world. To talk about Faerie. To get people used to the idea that we exist," he said.

"That's already happened," said Skye.

He looked at her, his face wrinkled up like it did when he was puzzled.

She continued, "New Age and Metaphysical stores. And has anyone been to Glastonbury in the last couple of decades?"

They all shook their heads, confusion covering their faces.

She rolled her eyes, "Where have you all been? There are maps to Faerie circles. Guides on how to find and talk to Fae. There's even books on gardening with Fae and which flowers please them. People build teeny tiny fairy houses; they must think we're all the size of bees. There's movies about Fae, books and stories about us. There's even music."

Egan said, "I had no idea. What would you suggest?"

Skye said, "Start with the people who are on the edge of believing and those who already do. There are lots of people around who still celebrate the high holy days. Samhain, Imbolc, Beltane and Lughnasah. Show up at their ceremonies. Not to bring a message, just to be present. To show we're still around. Show up at the Faerie mounds and the sacred wells. Take back the parts of the world that were originally sacred to us. Let ourselves be seen by those who would believe. Eventually, word of mouth will do the rest. We can perform subtle acts of magic, of healing."

"But those who believe in Fae are laughed at," said Adaire.

"Now they are. But it won't always be that way. I didn't say the changes in humans would happen overnight. But they will happen.

"I don't think we want it to happen quickly," said Meredith. "Humans are a paranoid lot and easily threatened. We need to come into their world slowly. Show them we can help them, that we're not an enemy."

Egan nodded.

"It beats trying to hide as a human," said Adaire.

Egan asked, "Would any of you be willing to go back out again?"

Meredith said, "There is no out anymore. We're all of us out now that the boundaries are gone."

"Okay then, out farther into the human world," he said.

Adaire shook her head. "I thought I was done, but I might be tempted to help restore some of the old woods that are struggling. Work with humans who are trying to accomplish that."

"I'll go," said Skye. "I trained as a massage therapist. As a healer. I can still do that. Take fewer clients, spend more time integrating myself into the healing community. Just tell me where you want me to go."

Meredith looked at her strangely. "You aren't happy here in Faerie?"

"The air spirits I've spoken to are…unaccepting. They don't want change. But things have already changed. They're being blind."

"I think perhaps you need to speak to more of them," said Meredith, quietly.

"If they show up, I'll be happy to talk to any of them, but where are they?"

Meredith shrugged, her face wrinkled with worry.

It was very apparent that the Court had emptied itself. Fled to somewhere. It wasn't just the air spirits. Water was gone and so was earth. Only the few fire spirits had remained and they'd become indolent. At this time, Egan's main support was Faerie herself, not the beings who dwelled there.

Egan said, "Has anyone seen Dylan?"

"He left once he healed me," said Meredith. "I suspect he had excess energy to drain off. He'll return once he's done that."

Fiachna spoke, "I've spent the last thousand years guarding the boundaries of Faerie. I've seen a lot of humans, but I was always under orders to hide from them. So I did. I think I'd like to be one of those who appear at the barrow mounds. Many of them need a lot of work, after the Fomorians. I'd be willing to do that, now and again. But I'd also like to spend more time in Faerie than I have."

"You can do both," said Skye. "Show up at the mounds when it's tourist season or a holy day."

"I cannot go," said Lassair. "I need to keep Aine safe within Faerie until she's older."

Egan said, "I will call a meeting of our people for tomorrow. For as many as are willing to come. I should have done it sooner. Too many are terrified of humans and are shaken by the arrival of the Fomorians. Faerie will never again be what it once was. We must grow and adapt. I just wish I had a vision of what that looked like."

"You will," said Lassair. "Trust that you will. You are still recovering from the spell that went wrong. Your mind will clear."

He nodded.

"I'm sorry," said Meredith. "I wasn't strong enough to attempt that spell. I should have known."

"There's nothing to apologize for," said Egan. "You did the best you could. No one had another plan. And it worked for the time being. Perhaps for eternity. We won't know until it no longer works. We will need to keep a vigil, always."

"And perhaps have a backup plan," said Meredith.

"Where have all the elders gone?" asked Adaire.

"I don't know," said Egan. He looked at Fiachna and Lassair.

Fiachna said, "I don't know. I've been outside, walking the boundaries. Ever since Faerie was closed. There were so few of us, then there was only me. I rarely came back in."

Lassair looked down at her hands.

"Many of them have withered away," she said. "I've been told that when Faerie was closed, the energy from outside was shut off. The elders who disagreed with the closing went off on their own, became solitary, not passing on their skills. The elders who chose to shut Faerie off found that the energy didn't flow like it used to. It had an end, like never before. Their old magic began to fail and they lost the desire to create new magic which would work within those limitations. They concentrated on glamour, it was easier than doing deep magic, like you did the other day, Meredith. I was lucky enough to have been taught by one of the elders before she withered away to silence. She still sits in the fire in our village, but never moves or speaks."

Lassair stopped speaking. Aine hugged her mother's arm.

"I wonder if the boundaries falling will revive the old magic," said Meredith.

"That would be something to see," said Skye.

"Something indeed," said Fiachna.

Chapter 42 · Dylan

Dylan woke to find a woman dragging him from the water and onto the shore. His fist was wrapped around a tree root. The root broke off and came along, still in his hand.

She was really strong.

He instinctively pulled free of her and got to his feet, staggering on the shore, trying to come back to the world.

"Are you okay?" she asked. "I thought you were drowning."

"I'm fine. I was just sleeping."

Her mouth dropped open. "Sleeping in the water?"

He nodded.

"I don't think I've ever heard about anyone who slept in water. Especially cold water." She paused, then said, "Well, there are those floatation tanks, but they're shallow and warm water."

She wore khaki shorts, a spring green T-shirt, socks and hiking boots.

She looked away from him, probably embarrassed by his nakedness. Humans could be that way sometimes.

Sitting down by a daypack, she took off her boots, emptying out the water. Her long blondish brown wavy hair was tied back in a low ponytail. She was quite the loveliest human he'd ever seen.

His hands itched to paint her.

She reached into her pack and pulled out dry socks.

"I'm really sorry," she said, taking off her wet socks.

"Sorry for what? Trying to save me?"

"Sorry for disturbing you. It's so annoying when people interrupt you, or wake you up."

"Thank you for the intent," he said.

She looked at his face, obviously avoiding looking at his naked body.

"Are you sure you're okay? You look a little pale."

"This is my normal color," he said.

Then she stared harder with those big brown eyes. He could tell she noticed his long braided, grassy hair, slightly larger than normal eyes and then the webbed feet and hands.

She backed up on the grass, trying to quickly put her dry socks and boots on.

"I'm not going to harm you."

"You're not human."

"No, I'm not," said Dylan, sitting down in the soft grass of the bank. Close enough to talk, far enough not to be a threat.

She stopped panicking and tied the laces of her boots.

"What are you then?" she asked.

"I'm Fae. A water sprite."

"That's not possible," she said, shaking her head.

"Well, I'm here, so it obviously is. You touched me, pulled me from the water. I'm flesh and blood, just like you."

"But Fae don't exist. Faeries don't exist."

He just smiled at her.

"I can't believe this is happening. I've been wandering around and found this area which wasn't on my map. I should've stayed back at the hotel and done the work I was supposed to do." She paused and said, "Now what happens?"

He shrugged. "I don't know. I've never been in this position before."

"Ookaay. Maybe I'll just stand up, pick up my pack, turn around and walk back the way I came. Pretend this never happened."

"You could do that," he said.

"And you wouldn't try to stop me?"

"Why would I do that?"

"Some human men would."

"Some would. Even when I spent time in human form, I was never one of those unevolved jerks."

She cocked her head and looked at him, "You spent time as a human? Why?"

"I was curious about humans. And there were political reasons I didn't want to stay in Faerie."

"Someone was trying to kill you?" she asked.

"Nothing so dramatic," he said. "I just didn't like what was happening. I chose to go out into the world instead."

"I didn't know Fae could do that. Crap, I didn't even know you existed. And why do you have an American accent if you're here, why not Irish?"

"I've spent the last thousand years as a human in the U.S. Where are you from?" he asked.

"I live in Seattle, but I was born in Colorado. I'm on sort of a working vacation."

"I lived on the Oregon Coast. Until recently."

"When you say on the coast, do you mean literally?"

"I was a human, renting a vacation cabin. Not in this form and I didn't live in the ocean."

"Wow," she said, shaking her head as if in wonder. "Just wow. A thousand years?"

Dylan nodded. He probably should consult Egan about talking to a human, but then again, this was how Faerie should be opened. One human at a time.

"You know you're inside Faerie?"

"How did that happen?"

"We had some problems with invaders. All our boundaries are down. They won't be going back up again."

"Why?"

"Again, it's politics. Times have changed. Those in charge have changed."

"So, it's not a magic thing. Do Fae do magic?" she asked, picking up her wet socks and beginning to roll them up.

In response he made her socks dry out instantly.

"Oh," she said. "You *can* do magic. I see. So why would you lock yourselves away?"

"I wouldn't. That's part of the politics. It's rather complicated. And humans haven't always been so blasé about magic as you are. It used to be a burning offense. Remember witches?"

"Yeah. Still, why shut away until now? This is the 21st. century."

"Politics. And not all humans are living in this century, are they? Not even all Americans are."

"No, I guess you're right. So, what happens next?"

"I don't know. My name's Dylan, by the way." He held out his hand.

"I'm Solange." She got on her knees, leaned over and shook his hand.

"You're still wet," she said.

"I'm a water sprite. I exude water as well as contain it. It's normal."

"What happens when you're being human?"

"I look and feel like a human."

"Huh," she said, staring at him as if she were reevaluating him.

"Would you like to see more of Faerie?" he asked.

"Would I be able to leave?"

"Yes, whenever you wanted to. Those old stories, they were about the time when Faerie was closed. It's wide open now."

"So, no tricks."

"No tricks. When you want to leave, I'll escort you back here, so you can find your way back to wherever you're staying."

"No kidnapping or me being gone from the real world for a hundred years?"

"No. And although you've never seen it, this is part of the real world too."

She sat silently for a couple of minutes.

Dylan looked around him. He saw a pair of dryads dance past, notice Solange and disappear in the trees.

"Okay," she said. "I'll come."

Solange stood, closed up her pack and shouldered it.

Dylan slid to his feet and they walked through the meadow grass towards the palace. He pointed out a few of the beings only seen in Faerie. Butterflies who flew backwards. Purple hummingbirds that fed from yellow flowers he didn't know the name of. An occasional dryad nurturing the trees.

There were others, but they were either too shocked or too shy to come out and be noticed.

They walked through the dappled shade of the birch trees. Then the sunny meadows filled with bees flying between white apple flowers. The blossoms were lush looking and the bees seemed happy.

The scents of Faerie seemed stronger with Solange, the colors brighter. Everything had more life. He'd lived over fifteen hundred years and never noticed apple blossoms. But then he'd never been with a human in Faerie.

He loved watching her reactions to seeing the magic which existed everywhere in Faerie. His eyes followed the emotions which flickered across her face, the melody of her laughter.

Was it because Faerie had been opened that the magic was coming alive again? Was it because of the energy that Lassair had transferred to him? He had no idea.

But it felt wonderful.

They walked half of the morning before coming to any dwellings. An earth spirit in one of them had left tables of freshly baked bread out in front. A gift. There were bowls of honey and jam to spread on the bread, as well as butter. And a pitcher of cool mint tea with glasses.

He and Solange stopped. Dylan didn't usually eat bread, he preferred fish. But he made an exception this time. He spread the soft brown bread with butter and honey. It tasted glorious, the rich and sweet flavors mingled together in his mouth. And the smell was divine.

"I've never tasted anything so good in my life," she said.

He sipped the tea and the mint danced around the lingering taste of butter.

Dylan bowed at the earth spirit who stood peeking out from behind a tree. He bowed back in return. Solange did the same. The earth spirit hesitated, then bowed back at her. Then disappeared back into his home made of columns of willows grown together into walls.

They continued on towards the palace. Since Egan had been made Luminary the center had changed. There were more stone houses. And more massive fires lit in empty spaces. Few stood around the fires, Dylan guessed they were all inside. It was as if Egan had brought fire back into balance with earth, air and water. That could only be good.

At the base of the hill upon which the palace stood a crowd had gathered. A huge new courtyard had been created between the stone road through town and the upper courtyard with the vault.

This courtyard was bordered by a ring of water over which bridges passed, although there were also places to wade through the water for those who chose to. Then a ring of tall, stately trees, Dylan guessed they were trembling poplars, but he wasn't that good about tree names. Inside that circle was a stone gathering place. A pillar of fire blazed in the center of it.

The courtyard was filled with Fae. He and Solange crowded in. The surrounding Fae were too busy looking at the center to pay attention to a stray human.

Inside the fire, on a large stone, stood Egan. He shimmered in the blaze and kept turning so that he could face everyone at one time or another throughout his speech.

"Many of you were made uncomfortable or were even perhaps injured when I first took over as Luminary. I regret that. The spell to imprison the Fomorians went wrong and all the elements were imbedded inside me. They've been released and I can now get to work."

He continued. "With the breaking down of our boundaries and the opening of Faerie, we must come up with a strategy of presenting ourselves to the world. We have many advantages that humans don't and we must be careful not to harm them. It's also crucial that they not come to fear us. They have enough weapons to wipe out the entire earth. And their politicians are not always wise enough to set weapons aside. We must find ways to live in harmony with our neighbors. These are not the same people as when Faerie was closed a thousand years ago. Nor are we the same. I believe humans have a great deal to offer us and we have as much to offer them."

"I'm asking those of you who wish to go out into their world and work as ambassadors to please come see me. There are several of us who've spent the last thousand years in the human world. We have ideas and information that you may find valuable. I'm also asking that should you find humans wandering into Faerie, that you show them kindness. Help them to find the way out or guide them to someone else who can help them find what they need."

"We have a lot of work to do. And a great deal of dreaming. To discover what we want Faerie to be now and in the future. I wish to bring Faerie into the present day and to regain what was a golden age for us. I need your help. We need the wisdom of the elders and the vitality of the young. Please feel free to come to the palace and talk with me. Once we were a people who believed 'Do no harm.' I hope as our powers increase through the re-opening of Faerie that we can again embrace that discipline. Faerie was closed out of fear. Let us never again act out of fear."

Many of the Fae cheered at this. Others remained silent. Dylan guessed those were the ones who still felt afraid.

The crowd began to break up and disperse. Out of the trees flew hundreds of ravens, who Dylan knew would repeat Egan's word to all those in Faerie.

Many Fae now noticed Solange's presence and were shocked. Some vanished or fled. Others gave a polite bow and left. Still others lingered, following her and Dylan up to where Egan stood, now out of the flame and on the stone courtyard.

Dylan had no idea what to tell Egan.

He simply knew that he wanted to stay with this woman.

And not just to paint her.

Chapter 43 ⟡ Egan

Egan stood in the new courtyard which was quickly emptying. He'd given them some things to think about. The breeze blew through the poplars, making their leaves whoosh and rattle softly. The sun shone down on the remaining Fae skin, leaving the air perfumed as if by exotic fragrances.

His mouth still reeled from the taste of Lassair's peppers which he'd eaten just before the speech. She'd been roasting again and had agreed to teach him pepper lore.

Egan noticed the human woman with Dylan immediately. Dylan was looking at her as if he couldn't take his eyes off her. It reminded Egan of the way his glassblower friend still looked at his partner of thirty years. The man had been completely besotted by his wife. And she with him.

Egan had never heard of or seen a Fae look like that. Humans yes. But then Dylan had spent a lot of time with humans.

Many Fae came up to him after the speech, asking what they could do to help. He had a schedule of gatherings in his mind. Tonight was for those who wanted to help within Faerie, help around the palace. Tomorrow morning was for those who wanted to plan how to work with humans. Tomorrow afternoon was for those who wanted to go out and do the work with humans. Tomorrow evening was for those who wanted to rebuild Faerie. The next morning was for those who wanted to work on a permanent spell to contain the Fomorians.

In between all those meetings he planned to meet with individuals, Fae who needed or wanted to work alone. Or those who just wanted to talk with him.

Finally, most everyone had left except Dylan, the human, and a group of Fae who were obviously curious about her.

"Egan, this is Solange, Solange this is Egan, our Luminary."

Egan bowed at her and she returned the gesture.

"What brings you to Faerie?" he asked.

"I was out hiking and I saw Dylan. I thought he was drowning and I pulled him out of the water. But he was only sleeping."

Dylan said, "I thought she might like to see more of Faerie. And to meet you."

"And what do you think of Faerie?"

"It's amazing. And you're all so different."

"So are humans."

"I don't think so."

"There's huge differences between Northern Europeans, Africans, Pacific Islanders, Native Americans and Australian Aboriginal peoples."

"That's true, but it seems like there's more, just between the two of you."

"We are opposites," said Egan. "He's water and I'm fire. But we're much more alike than we are different."

"I'll take your word for it," she said. "I can't see it."

"Perhaps you will with time," said Dylan.

"What does that mean?" she asked, looking at Dylan with an obvious suspicious look on her face.

Dylan said, "Well, now that Faerie's open, more of us will be coming out into your world. Humans will have more exposure to us."

"Oh."

Egan smiled. That hadn't been what Dylan had meant, but it was a good save.

"Three nights from now is the Solstice. We're having a celebration. You're welcome if you'd like to come," said Egan.

"What sort of celebration?" asked Solange.

"Music, theatrics, dancing, wine, food. The best that Faerie has to offer."

"Hm. I might just do that. Is it clothing optional? I'm not very good at nudity."

"No. On Midsummer we always dress. We wear the most ornate costumes we can make or find," said Egan. "And this Midsummer will be the most extraordinary in a very, very long time."

"Why?" she asked.

"Because we're alive and in Faerie," said Egan.

Dylan smiled at him and then at Solange.

Egan looked up to see Meredith, Fiachna, Skye and Adaire had joined the crowd.

This would indeed be a celebration to remember.

Author's Note:

I hope you've enjoyed Book 1 of *The Bones of the Earth Series*.

I've included two chapters of the second book - *Faerie Contact*.

Its release will be followed closely by the remaining books.

Faerie Contact
The Bones of the Earth:
Book 2

Bonus Chapters

Chapter 1 ✸ Clare

Clare switched the lights on in the store, wincing from the brightness. The exotic and unmistakable scent of Nag Champa incense filled her nose. Marcella must have been burning it last night.

As if most of the tourists could tell the difference between types of incense. Better to burn the cheap stuff for them.

That was not kind, Clare told herself.

She closed and locked the door behind her. The bell hanging near the top, chimed delicately.

Tea. She desperately needed caffeine. What flavor should she have today?

The store looked mostly tidy. Books on their shelves filled half the store. The rest was filled with crystals, candles, incense and burners. Display cases containing beautiful silver and gold jewelry, much of it decorated with semi-precious stones. Hand drums, painted and not, hung high on the sky blue walls. In one corner a rack held beautiful velvet capes in a rainbow of colors.

Near the check stand was a box containing lavender caramels for sale. For spur of the moment purchases.

The front display window was full of local interest books about Glastonbury Tor, the Chalice Well, and the White Spring. Designed to appeal to the tourists. Tourist season was drawing to an end, she'd need to change the window soon. Figure out what would appeal to the local villagers.

She needed to step up her game.

It was quiet in the shop, but not for long. She needed to get the music on and soon, things would be bustling. Mornings were always rushed for her. She should probably get here earlier.

Clare went into the back, flicked the hallway lights on and tapped in the numbers to turn off the alarm system. Then she went behind the main glass display counter, set the bank bag down on the chair and checked the messages. Only one, a supplier hoping to deliver today. She'd call back later when she could face talking to someone.

On the counter sat a pile of notes from Marcella. She always left behind notes about things that had gone wrong, customer requests and problems, and ideas for the store, many of them quite good. And a lot of clutter: books that needed to be shelved, a pack of open tarot cards, wrappers from the lemon candy that Marcella loved and three very expensive crystals. Which should be in the case.

Clare sighed. Marcella always left a mess when she worked. No matter how many times she'd been asked to clean up after herself.

In the back room, Clare hung up her purse on a hook, then her tan jumper over it. She took the kettle into the loo and filled it with fresh water. Then back out into the stockroom to plug it in. She pulled out a clean teapot and spooned some Irish Breakfast into it.

Clare pulled her current favorite mug off the rack. The turquoise one with the lovely painting of a green woman on it.

It had been a birthday gift from him.

Even though James was gone and her feelings for him still held an edge of bitterness, she loved the beautiful mug enough to overcome the connection.

She turned on some soft flute music for the store's sound system and glanced at the clock. Time to open.

Glancing longingly at the kettle, which was still heating, she glanced in the mirror, straightening the silver and jasper pendant around her neck. Pulled her tan blouse down and her tan slacks up. Ran a hand over her shoulder length hair, smoothing it. At least she looked neat and tidy. Like a well-run shop's owner should.

Clare went out to the front and unlocked the door.

She hadn't gotten her morning things done, but the tourists from the first buses would be descending soon. Opening the cash register drawer, she sorted the bills and coins into their slots and closed it. She slid the empty bag onto the shelf beneath the counter, tossed the candy wrappers in the trash and picked up the crystals, returning them to their cases. She patted them lovingly.

She noticed four other large crystals were missing from the case. Perhaps Jenny had sold them last night.

Clare shelved the books, then poured the hot water into the teapot, then went back in front to tidy up while the tea steeped. She managed to get her first cup poured before the first customers came in.

She perched on the chair behind the counter, cupping her warm mug with both hands. Cold hands, despite the sun shining outside.

Fall was coming. The mornings had a bite to them. Leaves were beginning to turn and the gardens she passed by on her way to work had that wan, worn out look they always had in late, late summer.

The three older women looked like typical tourists. Dressed in colorful pants with matching blouses and sweaters. Two of them carried small purses that hung like a backpack, only over one shoulder and the other had one of those silly fanny packs on. Probably practical, but funny looking.

The women passed by the books quickly, made appreciative sounds near the crystals and jewelry. Then they saw the fairy houses. They oohed and aahed over those.

Another group came in and began to make the circuit of the store.

Clare closed her eyes and inhaled the scent of the tea, sipped it and tasted the fullness of the fermented leaves and the richness of the cream. Lovely, just lovely.

"Excuse me," asked one of the women. "If I buy this, can it be shipped to the US?"

"Of course," said Clare. "You'll just need to fill out an address label and pay shipping."

She'd learned quickly that it was worth the effort to provide the service.

"Oh, then I definitely want it," she said, setting the fairy house on one end of the counter and going back to the display.

"Well, I'm going to get one too," said the second woman.

The third woman went back to the crystals.

Clare pulled out a pad of address labels. The bell on the door signaled another group of people coming in the door.

It was going to be a busy morning. She should have called the supplier back when she first got in.

Clare turned on the lights for the large back room and went to get some shipping boxes for the fairy houses. She noticed a trail of water on the floor.

Where did that come from?

She looked up at the high ceiling, but didn't see anything leaking from above.

She followed it to the door of the small empty room and opened the door.

The trail of water led into the room to the center of the floor.

The spare room was square and white, nothing special. It didn't even have windows. The floor was a dark wood, far from perfect, but serviceable. In each of the four corners sat the crystals missing from the case.

Clare picked the amethyst, white quartz, citrine and blue topaz. In the center of the room sat a large chunk of amber that she didn't recognize. Where had that come from? Maybe it belonged to Marcella.

She returned the crystals to their case out front, except for the amber which she put by the bank bag, checked on the customers and went back to find boxes. She'd mop up the water later, when there was a break from customers.

An hour later, Jenny got there.

"Sorry, I'm late. Me Mum didn't come on time. And Lucy's sick," she said, taking off her black jumper and hurrying into the back room to hang it up.

"Life happens," said Clare.

She tried to keep the judgmental tone out of her voice. It wouldn't help anything. She knew from long experience that whatever staff she hired had faults and none of them seemed to have lives as ordered as her own.

"I'm going into the office to make a few phone calls. It's been busy so far," she said.

"Brilliant," said Jenny. She busied herself with tidying up the remaining faerie houses and chatting with customers.

Jenny's short, dark hair was mussed up. She had a plump, matronly appearance and people warmed to her, confiding in her and asking her opinion. And Jenny willingly gave them her opinions in such a way that it was always polite and often funny.

Clare envied her ease with customers. She'd worked retail for decades and still had to work hard to be that friendly to strangers. She had so much work to do.

Clare went to the back, poured herself another cup

of tea, put a splash of cream in it and went into the small office.

The office was painted apple green. It had a wood desk, file cabinet and two wood straight chairs as well as a cushioned desk chair. There was a painting across from the desk, an oil of a pastoral scene. It looked down a hillside at hedgerows, a valley and the sky. The painting relaxed Clare. An electric heater stood in the corner. The room looked tidy and cozy.

Except that her desk was piled high with things which needed attention.

She made a note to talk to Marcella about the crystals and water this evening.

There were orders to put in, bills to pay, catalogs to look through to order more stock. Why did people still print catalogs anymore? Why didn't they just post them online and save a tree?

She returned the supplier's phone call, but he wasn't there. She left a message telling him, yes, please deliver.

Then called another supplier and talked her into giving the store a credit for their recent shipment of books, half of which had arrived bent, rumpled and torn. They'd been badly packed.

Then Clare called Kristin, the woman who made the fairy houses, asking for more. Kristin had another six ready, so she said she'd bring them by today. Which was good. Tomorrow was Friday and the weekends were often busy, especially just before school started. People taking last minute vacations because summer was ending.

At one, Jenny left for the day. She only worked part time.

Clare was sitting in the shop, flipping through catalogs and marking things to order when the door chimed again. The chime sounded different, lighter and more trilling, which made her look up.

In walked a woman with blonde wavy hair down to her waist. She had blue gray eyes and pale skin. She looked ethereal.

"Hello," said the woman.

"Hello," Claire replied.

"I'm looking for space to rent. I'm a massage therapist and energy worker and I need a workspace."

"And you have insurance and are all set up to work?"

"Yes," said the woman. "I've spent the last ten years working in the U.S. Seattle. But I'm from the west of Ireland, so I'm familiar with the requirements here."

"Ah, I thought I recognized the accent," said Clare. "You don't do acupuncture or any other medical things, right? You know they require more thorough licensing."

"No, just massage therapy and energy work."

"The shop down the street has a man who does what he calls Faerie Healing. He makes a good living at it."

The woman smiled and said, "I'll have to check him out. It's not my thing though."

"I'm Claire Grigson. I own the shop," she said, extending her hand.

"I'm Skye O'Hanlon," said the woman, shaking it.

"Do you have a clientele here?"

"Not yet, although I had a following in Seattle."

"What brings you here then? To Glastonbury?"

"I needed a change of scene. Seattle's a very big city. And I've always wanted to live here."

Another one. A pilgrim who wanted to soak up the vibes from the Tor. Or the Chalice Well. Or the Goddess or the Faeries. Or the ley lines. There were so many spiritual seekers who came to live here. But they always moved on, never stayed.

Well, that's why she had a business, wasn't it? A revolving customer base.

"Do you have a place to live?" asked Clare.

"Yes, I've taken a room in a boarding house in town. I don't need much space."

"Well, I'll show you the space. It's just off the stock room, so it's fairly quiet. My staff will be told when it's occupied they need to be quiet back here."

Clare led Skye through the stock room to the empty room in back. "We open at 10:30 and close at five. In the summer, sometimes we close earlier if it's really slow."

"That works for me. I really don't want to work evenings anymore. I did enough of that in Seattle."

"We all need to have a life," said Clare.

So where was hers?

Skye said, "I don't have a bank account yet. I really prefer to do everything with cash. If I have a customer who can't do that, can I have them pay you with their plastic and have you pay me cash?"

"I don't have a problem with that."

They discussed the rental fee and agreed on an amount. Skye handed over the first and last month's rent in cash.

"Is it possible for me to paint the room?" she asked.

"It needs it, doesn't it? I'll tell you what, I'll pay for the paint if you pick it out. I've never liked the white. It was an office before I bought the store. There are brushes, tarps for the floor and supplies over in the maintenance cupboard there. And a ladder in the corner," Clare said.

"Perfect," said Skye. "I'll be back this afternoon with the paint."

"You are on top of things."

"I want to get started and it'll take some time for paint fumes to go away."

Clare nodded.

Skye left.

Clare sat and began going through catalogs again. She needed to get all her holiday orders in soon.

Things were looking brighter. Clare had a tenant for the room she'd never let before. It had always been part of the plan, but she'd never gotten around to fixing it up or advertising. She'd only had the shop for six months and was still figuring things out.

This would help take some of the pressure off.

Shortly afterwards, Kristin came in, lugging a big box filled with Faerie houses. The middle aged heavy set woman didn't look like someone who would make Faerie houses. She had short cut dark hair, speckled with gray. Her baggy jeans and trainers were topped by a bright purple T-shirt.

People who made Faerie houses should look like the massage therapist who just left, not like moms.

Clare helped her unload the little houses and place them on the display table. Each one was unique. Most were made of wood, sticks and twigs formed into unusual shaped dwellings with artful decorations.

"I got two more finished, so there's eight," said Kristen.

"Oh, I love this one," said Clare.

The house had a tiny porch made from twigs with some sort of cone the size of her fingernail used as the top for each of the rails. The porch had a minuscule chair on it, with soft green moss for the cushion.

"That's a fun one," said Kirstin. "I am having such a lovely time making these."

"The tourists adore them. Keep making them please," said Clare, handing Kirsten cash for them.

"My pocketbook loves them too. Looks like we get to go out to eat tonight."

"Let's hear it for not cooking," said Clare.

She knew Kirstin was divorced with three boys. Cooking must really be something at her house. Boys were always hungry.

"So how's business otherwise."

"It's coming along. I've never had a store before, always worked for someone else. I'm not sure what to expect. Especially since tourist season is winding down."

"Then you should offer things for the locals," said Kristin.

"I've been thinking about that. What things do you think I should do?"

"Programs. Lectures. You know workshops."

"I don't have that much knowledge," said Clare.

"No one expects you to. But there are so many gifted people in the area who don't have a venue. You could provide that. Hold celebrations for the high holy days."

"Here, in the store? There's no room."

"I've seen the size of that back room. You're not using half of it. Do some rearranging and make a space back there. It wouldn't have to hold many, maybe twenty people. Make it an exclusive event. Charge a small fee to get in, enough to cover your costs and to pay the people leading it. You might have fun."

"I don't know anyone to ask to lead it. I've only lived here six months."

"I know several. I could introduce you. Tell me what sort of focus you want. I'll have you all over for tea and you can see if it's a fit. Make plans. It would be ever so much fun."

How long had it been since she'd had fun?

"Let me think about it. Figure out what it would take to make it happen."

"I'm not going to let this go, you know," said Kirstin. "Your shop is so much nicer than the others. I want to see it succeed. The places that keep going here cater to the locals as well as the tourists."

"Thanks. I will think about it."

"It means you'd have to step out of your shell. Take the lead."

She's already known that.

Buying and running her own store was a huge leap of faith in herself. But what Kirstin was talking about was even larger. It was taking her some time to screw up her courage.

"Well, I've got to run. Need to pick the boys up. Do some soul searching and really think about this."

"I will. Thank you," said Clare.

After Kirstin left, Clare went into the stock room. It would be easy enough to find the space in the store. She could decorate the walls with gauzy fabric and lights. Make it look magical, just as she had the front. After all, the front had been nothing but ugly bare walls when she moved in. She'd made it look beautiful.

So what was she afraid of?

Stepping out into the world and being seen by others? Then she'd have more work to do. It always happened that way.

Being responsible for whether other people were safe or even had a good time? She'd done that her entire childhood. Kept her sisters fed, clothed and helped with homework, while her parents drank themselves into a stupor every night.

Just remembering it brought back the sweet rot smell of wine. It made her stomach roil with nausea. She took a deep breath and sipped water from her mug.

She didn't want to be responsible for other people. She'd had enough of that and clearly wasn't any good at it. Look how both her younger sisters had turned out. Pregnant young, married young and always complaining about their lives, their kids, their husbands and being eternally broke.

Clara didn't want that life.

But what life did she want?

She wanted a life filled with love and joy. The love of a man who was her equal, not more, not less. She wanted to make a success of running her store. Enough money to travel. To buy what she wanted when she wanted to buy it. To pay her bills. To put a little away for the future. She had modest ambitions.

Clare glanced at the clock. Time to close up. She locked the front door, turned off the overhead lights, leaving just the twinkle lights on. Then emptied the register drawer and took the bank bag, money, checks and credit slips back into the office.

After she'd finished her accounting, Clare washed out her mug and set it on the rack to dry. Just as she was getting her sweater and purse, there was a knock on the front door.

Who could that be?

She peered around the corner to see Skye.

Clare unlocked the door.

"Hi, I know I'm late. It took me longer to get the paint than I expected. Can I just drop these off and then I'll start painting in the morning?"

"That would be fine," said Clare.

She let Skye in with her two cans of paint. Skye put them in her room and closed the door.

Clare picked up the bank bag, turned off all the lights and set the alarm.

Skye said, "I'm going out to eat, want to join me?"

Clare almost said no, then decided she should go. She needed to make some friends. Get out more. Her life was far too solitary.

"Where did you have in mind?"

"I passed a chip shop on the way back here and I've been craving them like crazy."

Clare's mouth watered at the thought. When was the last time she'd let herself eat something as unhealthy as fried chips and fish?

"Wonderful," she said.

Chapter 2 ❧ Skye

Skye bit into the fried fish and felt the heat. The fat and the rich tartar sauce fill her mouth. It tasted glorious. Food in Faerie was extraordinary, but sometimes humans did amazing things with it too.

She sat back in the hard chair and looked around.

The Spiffy Chippy was full of people on their way home from work. Every table was taken and there was a line out the door of people getting orders to go.

Clearly, this was the place in town to come for a quick meal.

It was in a new building, the colors were more conservative they would have been in a fish and chip shop in Seattle. A bold navy and white checked tile floor that made her eyes want to cross. She preferred more subtle patterns. Navy seats on the metal chairs and a shade darker table. Also made of smooth metal.

The smells were what had caught her attention as she'd walked past on her way to Clare's shop to drop off the paint. Deep fried fish and chips. The rich scents had filled the sidewalk outside as she'd passed by. Luring her in.

Across the table Clare ate her chips, delicately dipping them in ketchup pooled in the cardboard box her order came in.

Skye sipped the cup of hot black tea, feeling it warm her all the way down to her belly. How long since she'd eaten?

Probably not today. She'd been out pounding the pavement all day. Making sure her licensing and insurance were all in order and then looking for likely places to set up her practice. She hadn't eaten last night either.

She needed to remember to take care of this human body which covered her own. It was tiresome. Her natural physical body was so much easier to care for. Sylphs didn't need much. A little concentrated food. Some water. And a lot of fresh air. Wind was her element.

"So, how long have you had the store?" she asked Clare.

The woman seemed so unobtrusive. Probably in her mid-thirties, she had dishwater blonde hair that stopped at the top of her shoulders, brown eyes and she was dressed all in tan clothes that washed out any color in her pale skin. She was nearly invisible. And her posture said she liked it that way, slightly hunched over, only occasionally making eye contact.

Skye longed to have a session with her, make her open up and watch her blossom.

"I just opened it six months ago."

"Really? It looks like it's been there for ages."

"That's the look I was going for. I wanted to look established, but I also wanted to appeal to novelty. Have new displays float through a couple times a month."

"It's a lovely store."

"A few of the locals think I should hold events there, but I'm a bit torn about that."

"What sort of events?"

"Speakers, rituals."

"Why are you torn? It seems like a natural thing."

"It means putting myself out there in a way I've never done before."

"Change is always challenging for us humans. Even though it's a normal part of life," Skye said, lying about the "us humans" part.

"I know. I'm just afraid."

"Of what?" asked Skye.

She sipped her tea, loving the heat, feeling it to the core of her body.

"Of looking stupid, of failing, of alienating customers."

"Well, that sounds pretty normal. I will tell you one thing though, in my not so vast experience, when we're called to do something that looks like a big challenge to us, but it seems the right thing to do, then not doing it is like taking a step backwards. And if you keep going backwards, then that's just dying a slow death."

"I know what you mean. I've done that too often in my life. I really don't want to do it anymore."

Skye chewed on one of the chips, dipped in ketchup.

"Then it looks like you've already made a decision."

"I guess I have. I'm just afraid to move forward with it."

"You seem like a person who needs to plan and organize things before you move forward."

"Yeah."

"So, plan out a schedule. Figure out what you'd be comfortable with. Then adapt as needed."

Skye sent a small surge of energy in Clare's direction. A shot of courage and clarity. Not large enough for Clare to realize it came from outside of herself, but enough to make a difference.

"You make it sound so simple when you put it like that."

Skye laughed. "That's because I'm on the outside, looking in. My life is rarely that simple. It looks all muddled.

Her life was definitely not simple. A sylph masquerading as a human. An air spirit trying to ease the way for the rest of Faerie. To prepare humans for the shock that they weren't alone on this lovely green and blue planet. That they never had been. They had just in denial for several hundred years.

And now that Faerie's boundaries had been opened that transition needed to happen quickly. It couldn't take decades. And Faerie didn't want war. But humans were dangerous once cornered. They were a paranoid lot and easily threatened. At least that's what their history had been. Skye liked to think that as individuals they were decent. But as a group, they were pretty scary.

She, and the others who'd volunteered for the same task, had their work ahead of them.

Clare pushed her cardboard plate away from here.

"I'm stuffed. I can't remember when I last ate so much. And such unhealthy food. But it was wonderful."

"I know. You've got to do it now and again. Can't live on a diet of veggies and bland food," said Skye.

"No, you can't and I've tried for far too long. So let's do this again. Or maybe curry next time?"

"I love curry. Just let me know when it works for you. I have kitchen privileges where I'm living, but I'm not fond of cooking."

"Deal," said Clare.

After they finished and left the chippy, they walked through the crisp evening towards their homes. They both went the same direction for quite a ways.

The fog had come in, apparently that was common here. With it came a misting shower that felt cool. It soaked through Skye's hoodie and jeans in little time. She said good night to Clare at a corner, then turned and walked four more long blocks to the three story, brick boarding house.

The front door was still unlocked and she entered, closed it and went up the narrow stairs to the attic, passing by the crowded common room.

She unlocked the door to her room and went in, closing it behind her and locking it. She could smell the dried lavender she'd brought from Faerie, sitting in a paper cup near her bed. She sighed, releasing the stress of being around so many humans all day.

Privacy. Something she'd come to values while living among humans. It was so necessary for her survival. A place where she could hide and be herself. This small, cozy room at the top of the house was a sanctuary for her in the human world.

She switched on the small bedside lamp, stripped off her wet clothes and hung them over the foot of the metal bed frame.

Then she pulled on a pair of soft cotton pajamas with dragonflies printed on them and sat crosslegged in the big comfy chair in the corner, the peaked ceiling of the room slanting just over her head. The room felt warm and delicious, but it took some time to get her human body warm again.

She'd need to get some thicker waterproof clothes. She'd need this human body for some time.

Skye longed to leave her human body in the chair and go flying. But she worried about it, the temperature was still too cold. Humans were so fragile.

She missed the freedom of flying, of being light enough to float on the breeze. Skye missed the company of her own kind, but she was used to that. She'd only had other Fae nearby for the last several months. Before that she hadn't seen another Fae for nearly a thousand years. Ever since she'd left Faerie the first time.

But even when she returned a few months ago and the boundaries of Faerie were unraveled, the other air spirits had vanished. Fleeing from Egan's fire.

It had taken him quite a while to get his heat under control.

She missed her friends still in Faerie, even though they weren't air spirits.

Had all the other air spirits been devoured by the Formorians' winds? It wasn't the first time she'd considered the possibility. She sensed an emptiness that couldn't be accounted for.

The breezes and winds whispered nothing to her. As if they were lifeless. Never in her long life had she felt such a vacuum.

And it alarmed her.

Did the other elementals feel the same thing?

She was the first to venture out into the world after the fall of the boundaries and the imprisonment of the Formorians, the old gods.

Had they taken large parts of Faerie with them, as they'd planned?

She had no answers and a million questions.

Perhaps once she'd settled in and was earning money again, a trip back to Faerie would be possible. Just to check in and see if anyone else felt the same emptiness.

About the Author

Linda Jordan writes fascinating characters, funny dialogue, and imaginative fiction. She creates both long and short fiction, serious and silly. She believes in the power of healing and transformation, and many of her stories follow those themes.

In a previous lifetime, Linda coordinated the Clarion West Writers' Workshop as well as the Reading Series. She spent four years as Chair of the Board of Directors during Clarion West's formative period. She's also worked as a travel agent, a baker, and a pond plant/fish sales person, you know, the sort of things one does as a writer.

Linda now lives in the rainy wilds of Washington state with her husband, daughter, four cats, eighteen Koi and an infinite number of slugs and snails.

Visit her at: www.LindaJordan.net

Metamorphosis Press website is at:
www.MetamorphosisPress.com

If you enjoyed this story, please consider leaving a review at Goodreads or your favorite online retailer to help like-minded readers discover it. Thank you!

Get a FREE ebook!
Sign up for Linda's Serendipitous Newsletter at her website: www.LindaJordan.net